The Pigs Are Flying!

EMILY RODDA lives in Sydney, Australia, with her husband and four children; she combines writing with a full-time career in publishing.

The Pigs Are Flying!

Emily Rodda

CHAPT. 2
ECIA

Illustrated by Noela Young

AN AVON CAMELOT BOOK

This one's for Hal

AVON BOOKS
A division of
The Hearst Corporation
105 Madison Avenue
New York, New York 10016

Text copyright © 1986 by Emily Rodda

Text Illustrations copyright © 1986 by Noela Young

First published by Angus & Robertson Publishers in Australia and in the
United Kingdom in 1986 as *Pigs Might Fly*. This edition published by
arrangement with Angus & Robertson Publishers, Sydney, Australia.

Library of Congress Catalog Card Number: 88-2449
ISBN: 0-380-70555-9
RL: 6.2

Published in hardcover by William Morrow and Company, Inc.; for
information address Avon Books.

First Avon Camelot Printing: September 1989

CAMELOT TRADEMARK REG. U.S. PAT. OFF. AND IN OTHER COUNTRIES, MARCA
REGISTRADA, HECHO EN U.S.A.

Printed in the U.S.A.

OPM 10 9 8 7 6 5 4 3 2

CONTENTS

CHAPTER I
The Beginning

"I wish something would happen!" said Rachel.

Afterward, she would remember what she'd said and how bored she'd felt that rainy Saturday morning, and she would think: *That was really the beginning*. And her stomach would give a little jolt, and the tips of her fingers would tingle.

But at the time she didn't know what was in store for her. All she knew was that she was very bored. Bored with having a cold and being shut up inside the house, bored with all her books and games, bored with TV. She was sick of having a chafed, runny nose and a sore throat, and feeling hot and prickly and then cold and shivery in quick succession. And she was sick of the sound of the rain, drumming down on the roof of her room, beating on the concrete path, dripping from the gutters, gurgling down the pipes.

She heaved a dreary sigh and lay back on her pillows, staring at the ceiling.

"Something has happened," said her mother, tucking in the blankets and putting the books Rachel had been reading in a neat pile at the end of the bed. "The ceiling in Jamie's room's sprung a leak. He's been having a lovely time lying on his back and trying to catch the drops in his mouth. He must have been at it for twenty minutes. He's soaked, the carpet's soaked, Bluey's soaked, and now Chris is getting soaked trying to clean up!"

Rachel smiled, thinking of Dad battling the leak with Jamie toddling around insisting on "helping," with a dripping, blue stuffed dog tucked under his arm. Then she sighed again.

"I don't really mean that sort of thing, Mum," she explained patiently. "I mean something *interesting*. Something really *interesting*. Everything's always the same in this house lately. Get up, have breakfast, go to school, come home, play, have dinner, go to bed, get up, have . . ."

"Alice!" Dad's voice echoed down the corridor. His footsteps banged on the stairs.

"Okay, okay, I get your meaning," said Alice drily, ignoring the call. "You mean you think your life lacks excitement, adventure, romance, the challenge of the unlikely event, the unexpected. . . ."

"*Your* life lacks romance!" roared Chris from the hall. He appeared at the door with Jamie on his back, a bucket in one hand and a dripping cloth in the other. "What about mine, I'd like to know? I didn't ask for this sort of life! What would my real parents, the Duke and Duchess of Finklestein, think, if they saw me, their rightful heir, in this state? Alice, do you realize that Jamie's carpet . . ."

"Dad!" interrupted Rachel scornfully. "Your parents are Grandma and Poppy, not the Duke and Duchess of Finkleship!"

"Finklestein, please. And how do you know who my real parents are? For all you know. . . . Jamie, get down, darling, you're strangling me. Oh, that's better."

The doorbell rang.

"I go, I go!" squealed Jamie, and thundered off down the corridor.

"Don't fall down the stairs, don't fall down the stairs! Jamie, don't fall down the . . ." Screeching at the top of her voice, Alice ducked past Chris, missed the bucket by a fraction, and followed her son.

Chris shook his head. "A madhouse!" he sighed, and sat down on the end of the bed. "Too much excitement, if you ask me."

"It's the ordinary sort, though, Dad," said Rachel seriously. "I mean, it's how things are all the time. I want something different. Like—um—like, say, if the roof leaked and when you went up to fix it, you found a bird's nest with eggs in it, that we could watch hatch. That would be interesting. I read that in a book once."

"Yeah—well, we had that bat in the chimney. That was exciting," said Chris, a trifle grimly. He'd tried for two days to get that bat out. Finally, it had gotten itself out—very sooty and cross, into the living room, while they were watching television. He remembered the occasion well.

"Yeah, that's right! But that was ages ago. We don't seem to have anything like that now."

"No, fortunately not. How's your throat feeling?"

"A bit sore, but better," said Rachel, after a test swallow. "Dad?"

"Yes?"

"Maybe your long-lost parents, the Duke and Duchess of Finklesop, will leave you all their money."

"Finklestein," said Chris gloomily, stirring the muddy water in his bucket.

"Finklestein. Maybe they'll leave you all their money, and we can buy a houseboat and have adventures on it."

"You never know."

"Or we might find a treasure map under the house, or a secret room behind one of the walls, with a skeleton in it, or . . . or . . . a film person might see this house and want to use it for a film, like happened to Susie Swanning, or . . ."

"Oh, yes, or we might find a unicorn in the garden, and pigs might fly!" said Chris, tipping his head back and looking at the light through his eyelashes.

"Pigs can't fly!"

"Exactly!"

"*Dad! . . .*"

Thunderous, plodding three-year-old feet labored up the stairs. Jamie's face peered around the door.

"Sandy's here," he announced.

"Oh," said Chris, getting up. "I'll go down and see him."

"I want to come, too!" cried Rachel.

"So do I," said Jamie excitedly. "I want to

come!" He paused. "Where are we going?" he asked.

"Down to see Sandy, you gink!" laughed Chris. "Didn't you just tell . . . oh, never mind. Rachel, my love, you can't come. You're sick and you've got a temperature. . . . Now, don't argue, darling," he added, as Rachel's complaining voice rose. "Stay here. I'll send Sandy up to see you before he goes. Okay?"

"Okay." Rachel saw there was no point in arguing. And it was true she didn't feel very well yet. Even walking to the bathroom, her legs felt trembly and weak. But Sandy was a good cure for boredom, and she did want to see him.

Sandy was a sign writer. He painted curly, old-fashioned-looking signs for antique shops, big bold signs for butcher shops, fancy signs for dress shops, funny signs covered in cartoons for toy shops. He worked all over the city, wherever he was wanted. One day he'd be up a ladder, painting a sign high on an old brick wall; the next he'd be down on the pavement, lettering numbers on someone's front door, or painting the name of a park on a white board. He always had a story to tell about his latest job—the people he met, the places he saw. At home, for fun, he drew cartoons and illustrated maps—the sort of maps that had whales spouting in the oceans, and eels coiling in the rivers, and hordes of little people driving cars madly down the highways.

Sandy lived just down the road from Rachel's family, in a little house with a black railing fence. He had a parrot called Pol—a sulfur-crested cockatoo who adored him.

Now, interesting things happened to Sandy all the time, thought Rachel. Pol was a good example. About eighteen months ago, Sandy was working in his study upstairs when he heard a sort of tapping on the front door. He went downstairs, opened the door, and found this big white parrot standing there. The parrot raised its yellow crest (so Sandy said), fixed him with its beady eye, and said, quite clearly and firmly, "Give us a biscuit!"

"I was so amazed," Sandy had told them, "that I stood back, and it just walked in the door. Then it stared at me sideways, opening and closing its beak, till I got nervous and gave it a biscuit, like it wanted."

Pol moved in after that. She was never claimed by anyone, which was strange because she was a splendid, clever bird. Sandy always said she was, and Pol said it, too, very loudly, whenever anyone came up to admire her.

So that was one interesting thing that had happened to Sandy. But there were others, lots of others. Once he went to sleep in the zoo and got locked in. The keepers found him next morning, curled up asleep under a tree, with a little black duck roosting on his back. It complained bitterly when they woke him up and waddled all the way to the gate with him, quacking angrily and making grabs at his socks with its bill as if to hold him back. He said it was very embarrassing.

Rachel wriggled impatiently in bed. She could hear her mother and father laughing downstairs and knew that Sandy was telling stories and jokes in his soft, dry voice as they sat around the kitchen table. She wished he would come up and talk to her, and considered going to the top of the stairs and calling out. But, no—Dad had said he'd send Sandy up. They'd just get cross if she started carrying on about it.

As if to reward her for her self-control, there was the scrape of a chair being pushed back, footsteps in the hall, and finally the sound of someone climbing the stairs.

Sandy's bearded face popped around the door.

"Hello, madam," he said, and came in. He stopped in the center of the room and, with his hands behind his back, gave her a little bow. "And how are your germs today?"

"Germy!" said Rachel, wrinkling her nose.

"Ah—the little devils! Well, I have a few things that might interest you here, from below stairs. From your dear mother"—he produced a little bag from behind his back—"a midmorning snack to still the tooth of famine. From your respected father"—his other hand appeared with Rachel's school-drink bottle—"a cooling drink to soothe your parched throat. And"—he tumbled bag and flask into Rachel's lap and felt in his jacket pocket—"from me, a work of art, to please your eye."

Rachel took the piece of paper he offered her, looked at it carefully, and started to laugh.

"You've been talking to Dad about me!" she accused.

Sandy's picture, hastily sketched on a scrap of paper with a felt-tip pen, showed a tiny Rachel in pajamas, astride a unicorn in a broad, open field. In the sky above, several surprised-looking pigs floated. One was in the middle of a slow somersault. Its trotters stuck straight up, and it was smiling.

Rachel propped the picture against the lamp on her bedside table. She laughed again as the upside-down pig caught her eye.

"Thanks, Sandy. It's really funny. I wish things like that did happen to me. Well, not pigs flying, because that's impossible, but . . ."

"Maybe it's not impossible!" said Sandy, raising his eyebrows. "I always say nothing you can imagine is totally *impossible*. It might be *unlikely*, but that's as far as I'll go."

"It's all right for you to say, Sandy," said Rachel disgustedly. "Unlikely things happen to *you* all the time. But they never do to me!"

"Maybe," said Sandy airily, "that's because I'm the one who doesn't rule out the apparently impossible. Have you ever thought of that?"

"No . . ." said Rachel slowly, thinking it out.

"Well, why don't you try it sometime and see what happens. You never know, do you?"

Rachel looked at him carefully. He grinned back at her. Was he teasing, or not?

"Well, I'll try it," she said.

"Good! I recommend it," said Sandy. He walked back to the door. "Well, my little chickadee, I must be off. Enjoy your picnic."

"Where are you going now?"

"To the shops. Pol's run out of seed. She's nagged me about it the whole morning, and if I come back empty-handed I'll be in real trouble." He cast his hand up to his forehead in mock despair. "Off I trudge, in the teeming rain, all because of a cranky parrot. It's ridiculous!"

Rachel giggled. "See you, Sandy," she said.

He gave her a wave and a grin, and was gone.

Rachel sat back, still smiling, took a raisin cake from the paper bag, and had a bite. Then she flipped off the cap of her drink bottle. The cool orange drink slid down her throat. Sandy was funny. She looked again at his drawing as she finished her morning tea. The little figure did look like her. It was only a sketch, but somehow he'd gotten her hair, and her nose, and the way she sat, perfectly, in just a few lines. And the floating pigs looked so—so gloriously *piggy*.

She sighed and lay back on her pillows, the empty drink bottle still in her hand. Carefully she clipped on the cap, so it wouldn't get lost.

The house was very quiet. The rain beat down outside, and the gutters dripped. Rachel let her eyelids droop and watched the room through her eyelashes, as Chris had done. It all looked fuzzy and out of focus, and sort of magical, like the scene with the angels behind the gauze curtain at last year's end-of-term play. The light was like a star, hanging in space.

She turned her head so that she could look at Sandy's picture. It looked good this way. The lines darkened; the white spaces took on tinges of color. She concentrated on the picture, letting the rest of the room fade out of the background. There she was, little sketched Rachel, doing the impossible, in an impossible place. Nothing you can imagine is *impossible*, Sandy had said. It took a bit of thinking about, that. She let the words float through her mind. Nothing you can imagine is impossible. . . . Anything you can imagine is possible, somewhere, somehow. . . . Anything you can imagine . . .

The rain drummed on the roof. Outside, a car swished by on the streaming roadway. But Rachel, by now, wasn't listening.

CHAPTER 2
It Never Pigs But It Pours

Rachel blinked. Something had happened to the light. It had spread and brightened. Everything looked pale green. She blinked again and looked slowly around. This wasn't right! Her room had disappeared. Her bed had disappeared. She was in the middle of a broad, green field, in her pajamas, sitting astride a—

The unicorn turned its head and looked at her gravely. It snorted softly. Its golden horn glittered in the sunlight; its white mane stirred gently in the breeze.

"Oh, no!" whispered Rachel. "What have I done?"

The great muscles in the unicorn's back twitched, and it began to walk slowly forward, placing its feet gently on the tussocky green grass.

Rachel had ridden a horse only once before—and that was a Shetland pony. Only half a horse compared with this huge creature. She clutched desperately at the silky mane and hung on tightly with her knees. What else could she do? She couldn't possibly jump off. It was a long way to the ground.

The unicorn moved on quietly. And then Rachel heard the first, faint grunting. She knew where it was coming from, but at first she just couldn't bring herself to look. She screwed up her eyes and counted to ten. Then she opened one eye. Oh, no! She quickly shut it again. But it was no good. Seeing was believing, and she had to know the worst. She held on tightly to the unicorn's mane,

GOWER MIDDLE SCHOOL
LEARNING CENTER
7941 S. MADISON
BURR RIDGE, IL 60521

counted to ten again, gritted her teeth, and looked up into the blue sky.

The pigs were there, sailing plumply, pinkly, just above her, grunting softly to themselves. As she watched, one rolled over in a somersault and kicked its trotters at the sun with a little squeak of pleasure.

The unicorn pricked its ears and began to trot. Rachel held on grimly, bouncing on the broad, slippery back. No point in calling out—she couldn't see a single living creature who might help her. The pigs were having far too good a time even to notice she was there. She was in a strange field, in her pajamas, riding on a unicorn!

This must be a dream, thought Rachel suddenly. *Of course! That means I'll wake up soon, and there's nothing to worry about. It doesn't feel like a dream, but these things just don't happen in real life, so it must be.* This thought comforted her very much. She noticed her drink bottle sticking out of her pajama pocket. Somehow that comforted her, too. Something from home. What a shame it was empty. Her fright had made her thirsty.

The unicorn nickered warningly and quickened its pace. Rachel looked over its arching neck and saw that it had reached the crest of a hill and was heading for a small white house tucked away in the valley below. A pink blob bobbed around in the sky above the house. Another pig, for heaven's sake! And even as she watched, she saw that the wind was bringing more of them into view, tumbling and rolling. Little pigs, squealing and squeaking in excitement, medium-sized pigs, their legs spread out blissfully to catch the cool breeze, a few very big, whiskery old pigs, sailing along in majestic fashion, looking neither to right nor left. One great pig, the grandfather of all pigs, stood massively on the hillside, watching them with wise little eyes.

The unicorn broke into a gallop. Its hooves pounded on the grass, and its mane flew. The drink bottle flew from Rachel's pocket and fell onto the ground. She clung desperately to the unicorn's neck, hunched over like a jockey. She felt that any moment she would fall.

I suppose if I did fall I'd wake up! she thought to herself. *Maybe I should just let go.*

But somehow she couldn't bring herself to try out the experiment, and while she was still thinking about it and trying to persuade herself to be brave and take the risk, the unicorn slowed to a canter, then fell into a trot. They had almost reached the house.

*　　*　　*

The unicorn stopped and pawed at the ground. It nickered gently, and the muscles of its shoulders twitched. Rachel slid cautiously from its back and jumped to the ground.

The white house stood before her, its green-painted door firmly closed. A light glowed at one of the front windows, but the whole place had the air of being closed up tight, as if the owners had no wish to be disturbed. Rachel walked down the neat brick path and nervously put her hand on the old black door knocker. She looked nervously behind her. The unicorn was watching. It nodded its head and snorted softly through its nose in an encouraging way. Rachel turned back to the door, raised the knocker, and tapped three times.

"I'll go!" called a woman's voice inside the house. Steps approached the door, and it opened just a crack.

A plump old face framed with crinkly, wispy white hair peeped through the crack, and pale blue eyes gazed in vague surprise at Rachel.

"Excuse me . . ." Rachel began.

The door was flung wide. The old lady beamed and held out her arms.

"Gloria! You're here! Oh, I knew it! I said to Bertie, one piggy day, I said, you never know. . . .

Come in, dear, come in. . . . Bertie! Bertie! Gloria's here!"

"But . . ." Rachel stammered.

"Come in, pet, come in! Don't stand out there in the pigs, for goodness' sake." The old lady started ushering Rachel inside, as if protecting her from a hurricane.

Rachel took one last, confused look at the green hills basking under the perfect sky and stepped into the house.

"Thanks!" the old lady called nervously to the unicorn. "Thanks very much! We'll be all right now. No need to wait. Thank you."

The unicorn nodded in dignified fashion and began to walk quietly away.

"It's just as well to be polite, pet, isn't it?" the old lady said to Rachel in a lower voice. "They're that moody."

"Ah . . . I don't . . ." Rachel shook her head helplessly.

"What's going on? Enid? Have you got that door open? Are you bonkers, woman?" called someone irritably from the back of the house.

"Bertie!" exclaimed the old lady excitedly. "Look here! It's Gloria, Gloria!"

Rachel tugged timidly at her sleeve.

"I'm sorry, but I'm not Gloria," she whispered. "My name's Rachel."

The old lady turned surprised blue eyes toward her.

"Not . . . you're not Gloria? But . . ."

"Of course it's not Gloria, you silly old biddie! Don't hold the door open like that!" bawled an exasperated voice. A tall, thin old man stood, hands on hips, at the end of the hall. He beckoned impatiently to them.

"Come into the kitchen and, for goodness' sake, shut the door! Dear, oh, dear. Gloria!" He shook his head. "Gloria'd be a grown woman by now, Mum, you know that!" he roared. "Bring the girl in here!" He stomped off into the back of the house again.

"Oh, dear . . . I'm a silly old duck. It's this weather," said the old lady. "Come into the kitchen, love, and tell us what we can do for you. Come on. I'm sorry. I got you mixed up with someone else. See, I've been hoping . . ." She shook her head. "Anyhow, come out the back, and I'll get you a glass of milk. Eh?"

"Oh . . . um . . . it's all right," said Rachel nervously, glancing at the front door. She was convinced that both of these people were crazy, or at least had a few screws loose in their think saucepans, as Dad would have said. "I'd better . . ." She started walking back to the door.

"You can't go out in that, pet! It's blowing up to a real grunter. The pigs are up, love. Didn't you see? UEF 7 or 8 by now, I bet. Your mum and dad must be that worried about you. We'd better ring them up. If we can get through," Enid added doubtfully.

She bustled off down the dark hall and Rachel followed, feeling like Alice in Wonderland. She didn't understand any of this and didn't like it at all.

Ten minutes later, Rachel understood little more, but was feeling a bit happier. Enid and Bert's kitchen was a big, bright, white-painted room right at the back of the house. It was their living room, really, because easy chairs and a couch were arranged around a fireplace at one end, and the old couple obviously spent much of their time there. On one side of the fireplace stood a low cupboard with a television set on the top of it, and on the other side there was a bookcase full of old books, magazines, and china ornaments. There was no fire burning, of course, because the sun pouring through the windows was warm, but a basket of lavender had been arranged in the fireplace, and the soft, feathery gray leaves poked through the black bars of the grate, filling the room with a gentle, refreshing scent.

It was a peaceful scene, but Bert, the old man, looked worried and kept looking outside. The sky was full of fat, pink pigs now, clustering and rolling like round clouds through the blue air.

Rachel sat at the kitchen table, finishing the banana cake and milk that Enid had given her, and wondering why she felt so calm. A clock ticked loudly on the wall. It was a fancy sort of clock, with little doors, like the cuckoo clock at Rachel's granny's house. The clock said it was nearly a quarter to three! Where had the morning, and lunchtime, gone?

Enid, having accepted that Rachel wasn't Gloria, who was apparently her niece, had been very kind, but she was obviously a very unusual sort of old lady. She had fussed around finding Rachel something to eat. But it was a lot of trouble for her, because she kept forgetting where things were and then finding them in the most unexpected places. The cake tin, for example, turned up (finally) at the bottom of the wood box.

Enid didn't seem to think it at all strange that Rachel was barefoot and wearing pajamas, or that she had arrived on a unicorn's back. She just asked the usual grown-ups' questions, while she made herself a cup of tea—about how old Rachel was, and whether she had any brothers and sisters, and whether she liked school, and things like that. But then she forgot the answers to the questions and asked them all over again.

Bert stopped looking worried and started looking cross.

"And how old is your brother, dear?" asked Enid, for the third time.

"You've asked her that twice already, Enid!" snapped Bert. "Pull yourself together, woman! No need to give way completely!"

"Dear, oh, dear, I didn't realize," said Enid comfortably. "I'm sorry, pet. I had the door open too long and . . ."

"If I've told her once, I've told her a thousand times!" exploded Bert, finally losing his temper completely. "I've begged her—'Enid,' I've said, over and over, 'You know how you go. It's bad enough as it is, without going and making it worse by putting your silly head out in it!' Over and over I've said to her! It addles her completely.

No memory at all. It's enough to drive a man to drink!" He shook his fist at his wife, then ran his fingers through his thinning hair and tugged at it in fury.

Rachel, her mouth full of cake, sat frozen in alarm and embarrassment.

"Don't worry about him, love," said Enid, smiling and nodding to her as if nothing very extraordinary was happening. "The weather's gotten to him. He gets that cranky!"

"Cranky! Cranky! I'm just driven mad by you, you, you. . . ." Bert seized his hair again and pulled his head from side to side in helpless rage.

"He's a dear old thing, really," said Enid, fondly watching him. "But it takes him that way. In the off-season, Rosemary, he's the gentlest man that ever breathed, but . . ."

"Rachel—her name's Rachel, you old goop!" moaned the old man.

The clock whirred and Bert looked at it furiously, as if daring it to strike. But the little doors stayed firmly closed. He snorted at it.

Enid looked at him vaguely, the teapot lid in one hand and the steaming teapot in the other. "Why don't you see if the phone's working,

Bert?'' she said brightly. "Take your mind off it, love."

Bert stamped to the phone, which hung on the wall opposite the clock. Enid turned to Rachel. "It's bound not to, dear," she murmured, "but it's best to give him something to do while he's like this. Have you got any brothers and sisters, pet?"

"I heard that, Enid!" roared Bert, and began angrily tinkering with the phone.

Rachel's head was going around and around. How did she get involved in all this? Who *were* these people? What was wrong with them? They seemed to be saying it was something to do with the weather. The weather?

Bert slammed down the phone. "Dead as mutton!" he snarled, and then jumped violently as it rang loudly. He snatched up the receiver.

"Hello? Hello? No, this is *not* Fido's Favorite Dog Food Factory! Kindly get off the line, madam! . . . Well, that's not my fault, is it? Mitzi'll have to do without her din-dins, won't she? . . . Well, you should have gone shopping before it started pigging. . . . You . . . well, it was on the weather report this morning, and anyone with half a brain should've. . . . Yes, well, same to you with knobs on!" He banged the receiver down.

"The rudeness of some people!" he snapped.

Enid sighed. "You'd better go to bed, Reg," she said gently.

"Bert!" hissed Rachel urgently.

"Oh, yes, thank you, Rita. Bert, dear, go off and have a little snooze. It's the only way. Now, you know that."

"I don't want a snooze!" cried the old man, and stamped his foot exactly like a naughty toddler. "And what'll you be doing while I'm asleep, eh?

Wandering off, or forgetting the stove's on and burning the house down around our ears, I suppose. That'll be nice, won't it?"

"Don't talk rot, Bertie," said Enid calmly, putting the teapot lid into her apron pocket. "If I haven't burned the house down in fifty years, I'm not likely to start doing it now, am I? Besides, little Rose . . . um . . . Ruth . . . um . . . this little girl's with me, isn't she?" She turned to Rachel. "We'll look after each other, won't we, love?"

Rachel nodded nervously.

"Off you go then, dear. Have a nice sleep," said Enid.

Bert sniffed. "Well," he said ungraciously, "I might put me head down for a bit. I'll see." He hobbled past them and disappeared into the corridor without another word.

"He'll be much better when he wakes up, poor old chap," said Enid, putting the steaming teapot carefully into the refrigerator. "I blame myself. I was that excited, dear, thinking you were Gloria, that I never thought about the grunter at all."

Rachel could contain herself no longer. She *had* to know what this was all about.

"What's a grunter, Mrs. . . . Enid? Is it one of the pigs? How do the pigs make Bert cranky? Or make you . . . um . . . forget things, you know? . . . And, and, what is this place? How could pigs fly like that? I'm . . . I don't understand."

Enid stared at her, blue eyes wide and surprised in her soft, wrinkled face.

"My dear—oh—I never realized! Well, I never! Well, it never pigs but it pours!"

She came over and sat down opposite Rachel, her hands fluttering with excitement on the edge of the table. She leaned forward.

"You must be from Outside," she whispered. "Is that it? Are you an Outsider?"

C H A P T E R 3
I Want to Go Home!

"Um . . . I don't . . ." Rachel began, bewildered.

"You're not a local girl at all, are you?" whispered Enid. "You've come from Outside. Yes . . . yes, you must have. No local kid could possibly ask. . . . Well, oh, I'm that excited!" She held her hand to her heart. Her cheeks glowed. "Fifty years we've been in this house, and an Outsider's never landed on our doorstep once in all that time! Once every ten years, they say. I mean, that's the saying, isn't it? Very rare. Old Mrs.—oh—what's her name?—the lady down the road . . . anyhow, she had one, years ago, before Bert and I bought this place. Time and again I've heard her tell about her Outsider. And now I've got one of my own.

Oh, I'm that thrilled!" She clasped her hands and smiled triumphantly at Rachel.

Rachel's lip trembled. Suddenly it was all too much for her. "But . . . I want . . . I don't want to be here," she said, trying to keep her voice steady. "I want . . . I want to go home!" She felt her throat tighten and burn, and the tears start to fall.

The face opposite her grew sympathetic and concerned. The soft old hands fluttered nervously and then reached over and covered Rachel's clenched fists.

"Dear, oh, dear. . . . Oh, please don't cry, darling," pleaded Enid. She let go of Rachel's hands and began feeling in all her pockets. "Now, now! Oh, dear, I can't find my hankie anywhere. Now . . . oh, what's this?" She drew out the teapot lid and gazed at it with such comical surprise that Rachel began to laugh, rather hysterically, through her tears.

Enid laughed, too, with relief.

"That's a dearie, that's better. Now . . . um . . ." She made an obvious and enormous effort to concentrate, put the teapot lid firmly down on the tablecloth, and took Rachel's hands again.

"Now," she said. "They say that by tonight the grunter will have blown over, and you can have a good talk with Bert then. He'll be a different chap by then, you'll see. He'll know what to do. He's met Outsiders before, Bert has, see, and he'll know. But he'll be no good to us till tonight, so we'll just have to wait it out."

"Couldn't I just go and ask someone else?" asked Rachel desperately.

"Go . . . my dear girl, look at it!" Enid gestured toward the windows, through which green fields, blue sky, and hundreds of floating pink pigs could be seen. "Anything could happen if you went out in this! Don't you realize? . . . Oh, no, of course you don't, do you? I forgot . . ." Her voice trailed off uncertainly, and she bit her lip.

"See, love, you've got to understand . . . anything can happen in a grunter—a real grunter like this one. The trouble is, I'm that addled at present I'd never explain it so you'd . . ." She concentrated fiercely on the problem, and suddenly it was as if a light was switched on behind her eyes. They brightened and widened, and she sprang to her feet.

"Of course! I've got it, Rita. Now, if I can only find it. Come over here, dear."

Enid bustled toward the fireplace, beckoning eagerly, and Rachel followed her.

"Now, look here," said the old lady, kneeling painfully by the bookcase. "There's a book here that'll tell you all about it. An old one of . . . of . . . my husband's, you know, who's just gone to put his head down. He's the reader in the family. Now, where is it? . . . um . . . now, it was on the bottom shelf. I'm sure I saw it only last . . . oh!" A thought struck her, and she turned anxiously to Rachel. "You can read, dear, can't you?"

"Of course I can!" said Rachel indignantly.

"Well, you know, I wasn't sure . . . well, that's good." Enid turned back to the bookshelf. "Now, what's this? Oh, *The Cricket of Oz*, I used to love that . . . um, *Maisie Poppies*, *Grime's Piggy Tails*, dear, oh, dear. Oh, where is it? Aha!"

Triumphantly, Enid pulled a large, thick book from the shelf and handed it to Rachel. The cover was rather faded and brittle, but the title still showed clearly, inside a circle of red and yellow question marks. *The Child's Complete Book of Knowledge* it claimed boldly, and then, in smaller letters: *All About the World We Live In*.

"Bert's kept all his old books," said Enid proudly. "Well, it just goes to show, everything comes in. We always thought they'd be nice for Gloria, see? It just goes to show . . ." Her voice trailed off. Her kind, vague old face fell a little, and her blue eyes looked sad. "Gloria loved her books," she said.

Rachel stood awkwardly by her, not knowing exactly what to do.

The clock on the wall whirred again, and suddenly the doors flew open and a madly smiling little pig with a curly tail popped out. "Oink, oink, oink," it squealed, and shot back inside. The doors snapped shut.

"Help me up, dear," said Enid suddenly. "The old bones aren't what they were. Oh, dear!" She

scrambled to her feet, brushed at her knees to which threads of fluffy carpet clung, and glanced nervously at the clock.

"Well, it's behaving itself, anyway," she said. She tapped the book with her finger and smiled at Rachel encouragingly.

"You sit down here in the sun and have a read of this, love. It'll tell you all about us, and then you'll be that much further ahead for when Bert wakes up. Okay?"

Rachel nodded and looked at her. "Gloria is your niece, is she?" she asked shyly.

"Yes, love." Enid blinked quickly and smiled sadly. "My sister Pearl's girl. Pearl married my husband's brother, you know. Pearl and me, we met the boys at a dance, and she fancied one, and I fancied the other. Funny, wasn't it? Happened in a grunter, of course," she added wryly. "So, 'course, when Gloria was born, well, she was our niece twice over, see? We never had any kids of our own. She come to live with us when Pearl and Fred died in an accident. More like a daughter than a niece she was, to us." The blue eyes were far away.

"Dear little thing, she was. She'd been with us

two years when she went. Only five years old. Much younger than you, dear, of course, but she had fair hair and brown eyes, just like you. That's what put me wrong, see? When I saw you at the door I forgot Gloria'd be a grown-up woman by now. I just thought: 'Well, look at that! A grunter took her away, and a grunter brought her back. I always knew it would happen,' I thought to myself. But . . ."

"A *pig* took Gloria away?" exclaimed Rachel in horror, imagining little Gloria being bowled away in the sky between the trotters of a big pink pig.

"No, no, pet. Not a *pig*. A *grunter*. Oh, see, that's what we call it when the UEF goes up and the pigs fly—like now."

"The . . . UE? . . ." Rachel was lost. But Enid was lost, too, in memories. Obviously, the weather only affected part of her memory, the bit that handled the present. Her memory of the far past was crystal clear.

"Ah, yes," she said sadly. "It was a day just like today—twenty years ago this year. Blowing up a real grunter, it was. Force 8 predicted, but Bert and me had closed up the windows and doors like always, and we were safe inside. Well, he was a

bit cranky, like he gets, and I was, you know, a bit
wafty like *I* get, but we were all right and getting
ready for tea. But Gloria—she was worried about
this little kitten she had. She couldn't find it anywhere, see, and she hated to think about it being
outside in the weather. I mean, animals don't feel
it like we do, dear, but it does upset them, 'spe-
cially when they're young. So Gloria slipped outside, to try and find it."

Enid shook her head. "Naughty girl. She'd been
told and told, but she was only a little thing,
and . . ." Her voice trailed away.

"What happened?" asked Rachel awkwardly.

"Well—well, we lost her, see, pet," said Enid
vaguely. "We never saw our Gloria again."

"Oh!" Rachel was stunned. "Oh . . . I . . ."

Enid patted her hand. "Ah, well," she said.
"Sometimes these things happen. We miss her,
Bert and I do. But, look, she's happy wherever
she is, and that's what counts."

Rachel swallowed. "You mean . . . she died and
went to heaven?" she said.

Enid looked at her, aghast. "Good heavens, pet,
what put that idea into your head? Oh, no, I know
Gloria's okay, and not too far away, either. Her

life light's still burning bright as bright, in her room. I'm sure it's gone a bit brighter, just in the last week. Bert doesn't think so, but I . . ." She glanced at the amazed Rachel.

"Don't tell me you don't have life lights Outside?" she breathed.

Rachel shook her head.

"But—but that's *terrible*!" exclaimed Enid, looking scandalized. "How do you get on, then? How do you keep track of each other? I mean, if you wander off in a grunter and join a circus or something, how do your parents know you're all right?"

"They . . . they don't," wailed Rachel, overwhelmed again by homesickness. "We don't have grunters where I live. We . . . we don't wander off and join circuses and things like that. We stay home, with . . . with our families . . . if we can. . . ." The tears began to fall again.

"Dear, oh, dear. Poor little pet. Now, now— we'll get you home, Bert and me. You'll see." Enid put her arm around Rachel's shoulders, her kindly face all wrinkled up with concern. "You stop that crying—that won't get us nowhere, will it, love? Be a brave girl." She searched again for her handkerchief and finally dabbed at Rachel's tears with the hem of her apron. She led her to an armchair.

"Now," she said. "Curl up in this comfy chair, see? And have a good read and find out all about us. That's the best thing for you to do. I'll sit here and keep you company."

She settled down into the opposite armchair with a little sigh. "I'm glad to have a sit-down, to tell the truth. These grunters take it out of you. I'm glad the season's nearly over. We'll have a cold tea," she added vaguely. "Safer." She took some knitting from a bag by the chair. It was dark green and looked like the sleeve of a sweater. She counted the stitches and began clicking the needles.

Rachel sniffed, took a shuddering breath, wiped her eyes with the backs of her hands, and sat down in the chair, the book heavy in her lap. She turned to the back to find the index, then she checked through the index till she found the words beginning with "g." ". . . garbage disposal . . . garages . . . geese . . . gold mining . . ."

The clock whirred. The little pig shot out of its house and oinked piercingly fourteen times. The doors snapped shut again, and the clock hands moved on twenty minutes.

"Oh, dear," sighed Enid from her chair. Then she shrugged comfortably. "I'm glad Reg . . . er, Bertie's in bed," she said to Rachel confidingly. "That makes him so mad!" She went back to her knitting.

Rachel stared at the clock, and then at Enid, who was happily knitting a bright pink stripe into the shoulder of the dark green sleeve, and shook her head slightly, to see if the confused feeling inside it would go away. It didn't. She turned back to the book.

". . . government . . . grass . . . griffins" (griffins?!) . . . ah, there it was, "Grunters. *See* Unlikely Events Factor, p. 432."

Quickly she turned the thick pages of the book until she found the one she was looking for. She began to read.

CHAPTER 4
What the Book Said

UNLIKELY EVENTS FACTOR (UEF)

As we know, the weather affects all our lives. For centuries, human beings have tried to understand and control this aspect of nature without very much success, and even today it must be said that understanding, let alone control, of UEF storms (commonly known as "grunters" because of the effect they have on the swine population) is still not a reality.

The UEF storms (usually measured according to severity on a scale of 1 to 10) have many adverse effects on the economy. In the "grunter" season, when the storms occur frequently and UEFs of Force 8 and 9 are common, many working hours are lost due to the storms' startling effect on people's personalities, reliability, and efficiency in the workplace and in the home.

Rachel looked under her eyelashes at Enid, who was humming to herself as she knitted bright pink fingers onto the green sleeve. The book went on:

> It is well documented, furthermore, that strange accidents, coincidences, the malfunction of machinery, strokes of good fortune, and other "unlikely events" tend to occur during these storms. . . .

The clock whirred threateningly, and Rachel held her breath, but the little wooden pig did not appear.

> The most obvious visible sign of a UEF storm is undoubtedly the presence of pigs in the sky. It is not known exactly why the UEF causes pigs, and only pigs, to defy gravity and take to the air, but it *is* known that the more airborne pigs there are, the higher the UEF Force is, and the greater is the need to stay indoors, so exposing oneself as little as possible to the often bizarre effects of the Factor when breathed or absorbed through the skin in any quantity.

So that's why the windows are all shut tight, thought Rachel, looking around. *And poor old Enid's gotten more addled than usual because she stood in the open doorway talking to me when I arrived. I suppose we let a lot of UEF into the house in those few minutes. Enough to make Bert so cranky he had to go to bed!* She turned back to the book and read on.

> Most of you will know of people who have wandered away from their homes in UEF storms, having been imprudent enough to stay outside for too long. (*Like Gloria!* thought Rachel.)
>
> Some of these people return within a day or two. Others forget where their homes are and begin life again elsewhere. They have only vague, pleasant memories of the past, and as there are many thousand such cases each year, they are readily adopted into their new communities. Most go on to lead happy and useful lives.
>
> It should be pointed out, however, that the large costs involved in the constant organizing of search parties to comb the country for missing persons, not to mention the disruption to homes, families, and businesses when family members or valuable employees disappear without warning, is most injurious and should be avoided if at all possible. Practice the UEF Safety Drill at home and at school, take shelter at once at the first sign of pig-rise, and *never* go out in a grunter.

What a place! thought Rachel. But she saw now why Enid and Bert accepted Gloria's absence sadly but so calmly, as if it were just another fact of life. Obviously, people moved around a fair bit in this mixed-up world. Bert and Enid missed Gloria, but they knew she was happy and contented wherever she was, and that, to them, was the most important thing.

It is interesting to note (the book went on) that, until the beginning of this century, it was widely believed that the "flying pigs" actually *caused* the disturbing effects on people and the environment. That is, it was believed that if the pigs could be kept on the ground, the surprising events that characterize a UEF storm would not occur. This false and superstitious belief led to the disastrous "trotters on the ground" fad that swept the country after it was introduced by the then minister for weather, Dr. Gerald S. Pimplebottom.

Dr. Pimplebottom urged that all pigs be confined in low-roofed shelters and netted sties, to prevent the animals rising into the air. A countrywide campaign succeeded in containing the entire pig population just before the beginning of the official "grunter season." Dr. Pimplebottom announced that his government had solved "the problem of the age," and predicted an era of unprecedented prosperity for the nation.

"Leave your windows open, your doors ajar," he said confidently. "The skies are clear. The grunter menace is from today ancient history." He and the prime minister, Lady Sonia Mingus, celebrated the first day of the season, as you will see in the historic press photograph at left, by having a tea party in the open air in the grounds of Parliament House.

Unfortunately, of course, the containment of the pigs simply meant that when one of the biggest UEF storms in the country's history blew up on the third day of the season, it arrived unseen and totally without warning. As no pigs were able to rise, the UEF was not measured, but it was believed to have been Force 10.

Havoc was created in schools, offices, and factories across the nation, where none of the safety precautions usually employed in the grunter season had been observed.

■ It is estimated that ten thousand people left their places of work in the belief that they would prefer to be working elsewhere, or not working at all. Many of these people were later found selling drinks on the beach, training as circus clowns, and digging for gold in the mountains.

■ Schoolchildren at fifty-seven schools expelled their teachers and went on holiday. At forty-eight other schools, by contrast, children began to work so hard that they covered a whole year's curriculum in one day. Many teachers at these schools suffered nervous collapse. Some never recovered from the shock and were forced to go into early retirement.

■ The small town of Sweetlip was devastated when

the ice-cream factory that provided its main source of employment went into overproduction, and chocolate marshmallow sundae burst its containers and flooded the main street. The entire population of the town, and a hundred and twelve dogs, suffered from severe bilious attacks and frostbite as a result of the tragedy.

■ The Footsville shoe factory produced twelve hundred purple, high-heeled left shoes in six hours during the height of the storm. The foreman, Mr. Eric Sole, said afterward that it had "seemed like a good idea at the time."

■ Hundreds of sets of twins, triplets, and quadruplets were born at maternity hospitals all over the country on this one day, sending population figures soaring and leading to severe overcrowding in child-care centers and schools in following years.

■ Members of Parliament unanimously passed a law that every citizen over the age of ten years had to wear a bag of fish and chips on his or her head in public at all times.

■ Many pig owners were deafened for several days, due to the earsplitting squeals of their captive animals, which were apparently enraged because they were being prevented from taking to the air. Some pigs even turned on their owners. Mrs. Freda Moan of Snoutly was severely bitten on the elbow by her six-year-old boar, Henry. "Henry's been like a son to me," she said bitterly from her hospital bed, "and this is how he treats me!"

On the day following the disaster, the prime minister held an emergency cabinet meeting. She later released a statement requesting that all pigs be immediately released. It had been proved once and for all, she said, that the flying pigs did not *cause* the UEF but were an *effect* of it. Furthermore, she said, pig-rise provided a valuable early-warning system that had enabled people for centuries to prepare for UEF storms and take measures to lessen their effects. In the same statement she repealed the Fish-and-Chips Act, saying that it had proved impractical.

Dr. Pimplebottom was not present at the emergency meeting. He had rushed out of Parliament House the day before, apparently giving chase to a large pelican that had entered the members' canteen and made off with his lunch (sausages, chips, peas, and rice pudding). He never returned to political life, and it is believed he ended his days working as a model train driver in the Blissikins Amusement Park.

Since the Pimplebottom Theory Disaster, there has been some success in predicting UEF storms, and weather bureau research is continuing. Every household, however, should maintain a private pig as an early-warning signal. A government subsidy is available to assist those of modest means who may have difficulty in buying and feeding their animals.

Rachel closed the book and sat staring at the question marks on the cover. She shook her head slowly and glanced over at Enid.

The old lady was dozing, her knitting in her lap.

The shoulder of the dark green sweater sleeve now sprouted a bright pink glove, with six fingers.

The clock whirred dangerously, but did not strike.

Rachel walked over to the window. Like huge pink balloons, the pigs bobbed in the sky. There were so many now, she couldn't count them. How long would the storm last? she wondered. Enid had said that it would be over by nighttime. Perhaps, then she could try to get home. What she had read in the book made it clear that she would have to stay where she was until the grunter was over. Anything might happen out there.

At least she knew that there had been Outsiders here before. And when Bert woke up, he'd be able to tell her something about them, Enid had said. Perhaps the book could, too! She ran back to her chair and looked up "Outsiders" in the index. Yes, there it was. She turned to the right page. There was only a short paragraph:

OUSIDERS

This is the name given to occasional visitors from another world, the location of which is unknown.

Little is known about these people, who always appear suddenly just before, or during, a UEF storm, Force 8 or above (*see* Unlikely Events Factor, p. 432) and are apparently unaware of the means by which they arrived. Folk wisdom has it that Outsiders appear about once in every ten years. It is interesting to note that UEF storms are either unknown or very uncommon Outside, and Outsiders seem to be affected only slightly by the UEF, even when exposed to it in full strength.

Well, thought Rachel. *That's not much use! Except to explain why I'm not cranky, or forgetting things, or wanting to join a circus, or anything like that. Maybe Outsiders aren't affected by the UEF because they've been made immune by the whole business of getting here! I mean, what more unlikely thing could happen to you than that?*

The clock whirred. The little pig sprang out of its house and squeaked piercingly four times.

Enid's eyelids fluttered and she stretched. "Oh," she yawned, "I must have dropped off! Dear, oh, dear!" She caught sight of Rachel and blinked, her eyes wide with surprise.

"Gloria!" she cried. "Gloria, you're here! Oh . . ."

"No . . . no . . . I'm Rachel," said Rachel quickly. "I arrived before. Um . . . do you? . ."

Enid's face suddenly lost its bewildered look.

"Oh, yes, pet—I'm sorry. Yes, I remember . . . um . . . I think I remember . . . yes, I *do* remember, of course I do. You came with the grunter. Is Dora down yet?"

"Dora? Um, I don't . . ." said Rachel, looking around. Was there someone else in the house she hadn't met yet?

Enid put her knitting down and heaved herself out of her chair. She toddled to the window and looked out.

"Oh, no," she said. "There she is, bless her heart. Still up. Glory, what a storm!"

Rachel ran to look.

"There's our Dora," said Enid proudly, pointing. "The one with the green bow . . . just to the left of that tree. See her?"

Rachel's eyes followed Enid's finger. Yes, there was Dora—a broadly smiling pig with a green ribbon around her neck, bobbing upside down in the air, trotters pedaling gleefully in the breeze.

"She doesn't go up too high, these days, Dora doesn't," said Enid fondly. "She's not as young as she was. Still, she'll be tired out tonight, the way she's going. She has a whale of a time up there with all her mates. Look at her, will you?"

"Dora still up, is she?" said Bert's voice from the door. Rachel jumped. Oh, no. Not bad-- tempered Bert again. She watched nervously as he strode to the window and looked out.

"Ah . . ." He shook his head. "Fool things— look at them. Kicking up their heels while we're stuck in here. The veggies want watering, too. I'll have to get out and do them sometime today or they'll be dead as mackerel."

Rachel looked at him carefully. He still seemed a bit out of sorts, but the really scary bad temper had disappeared, and his face had lost its fero- cious look. His nap had done some good, then.

"Still, they're lower, I reckon, Enid," said Bert, putting his hand on his wife's shoulder. "Another few hours and we'll be all right." He turned to Rachel. "Then you can be getting on home, lass, can't you?" he said, quite kindly, really.

Rachel looked at Enid for help, but the old lady smiled back at her vaguely. She must have forgotten that Rachel had come from Outside.

"Cat got your tongue, miss?" snapped Bert, suddenly irritable again.

"No . . . sorry." Rachel swallowed and blinked fast to keep back the tears that threatened to fill her eyes again. She cleared her throat and took a deep breath.

"Mrs. . . . Enid said . . . you would help me get home," she whispered. "I don't live here. I'm . . . um . . . the book says, Enid says, I'm an Outsider, and . . ."

"*What!*" Bert's eyebrows shot up. "You're pulling me leg! Enid, what's this?"

Enid jumped. "What, Reg?" she murmured, looking at him in surprise.

"What's this about Outsiders? Pull yourself together, you scatty woman!"

Enid stared at him, and then her face cleared. "Yes!" she cried. "Oh, I remember! Yes! Bert, isn't it thrilling? This little girl's an Outsider. Our first Outsider in all these years." She put her arm around Rachel's shoulders and beamed at her husband. "She needs our help to get home, love, and I told her you'd do everything you could. I said you knew all about Outsiders. She *is* one, Bert. She didn't know about grunters, or UEF, or anything. And she wants to get home, poor little pet. Did you know they don't have life lights Outside? Her mum and dad must be frantic!"

"Well, strike me lucky!" breathed Bert, gazing, fascinated, at Rachel. "I can't get over it! Come and sit down here, love, and tell us all about it, eh?"

"I'll make a cup of tea," said Enid happily. "If I can find the teapot!"

CHAPTER 5

We've Got a Problem, All Right

When Rachel had finished her story, and Bert had asked her all the questions he had to ask, he cleared his throat, put his hands on his knees, and looked at her thoughtfully.

Rachel waited anxiously.

"Well, we've got a problem, all right," he said at last.

Rachel's face fell. This didn't sound too hopeful.

"But—I thought you knew all about—um—Outsiders," she said reproachfully. "Enid said . . . I hoped you'd know what to do with me, to get me home."

"I don't know *all* about anything, lass," said

Bert rather coldly. "I'm just a farmer. Not some university professor or something."

"But you can help a bit, can't you, Bertie?" coaxed Enid, from the other end of the kitchen.

"Oh, remembering my name now, are you?" retorted Bert. "Bully for you!"

"Now, look, Albert Beddoes!" flashed Enid, her face going pink all over. "Don't you go too far! I've been very patient with you and . . ."

He held up his hands. "Sorry, sorry. Grunter talking, love. Sorry." He turned to Rachel. "Now, Rachel," he said, much more gently, "as I see it, we should get some advice from a couple of people I know in town, who've actually spent a lot of time with Outsiders before. Like, I've read about them, and talked about them, and even met one once, but, see, I've never helped one get back Outside before."

"Do they . . . do we . . . *always* get back?" asked Rachel in a small voice.

"Well, look," said Bert carefully. "Put it this way . . . ah . . . there are some, there've been some, over the years, by all accounts, that haven't *wanted* to get back. They like it here, see, and they stay on, and after a while they forget they ever lived anywhere else, and . . ."

"Oh, *no!*" cried Rachel. "Oh, no! But I've . . ."

"Oh, but you're different from them, dearie," Enid put in hastily, glancing warningly at Bert, "because you've got your people to go back to and all."

"I'd *never* forget," wailed Rachel. "I wouldn't want to ever forget. . . ."

"Of course not, love," said Bert, patting her knee. "What I was going to say was that some of you people are that way, but on the whole, Outsiders do want to go back Outside, and the fact is, we think that somehow they make it. Some of them stay a few days or a few months. One Outsider bloke I knew of stayed around for a year—worked at the bank in town, he did. But in the end they all go, quite sudden. And we think—the books say so, too—that they go back Outside."

"But . . . you don't know they do," said Rachel hopelessly. "They could just have gone out in a grunter and gotten mixed up and gone somewhere else Inside to live—like—like Gloria did."

"Ye-es," admitted Bert, "but generally Outsiders don't get muddled up by the UEF like we do. Not till they've been here years and years. So, chances are they don't just wander off. Chances are they suddenly work out how to get home, and they just go." He paused. "Must be, you know, very . . . peaceful, Outside," he said, almost wistfully.

"Well—in a way," said Rachel thoughtfully. "Yes, well, usually it is—at least, compared to here. Not so many funny things happen all at once. But funny things do happen sometimes, and interesting things. I like it when they do. I mean, here they never stop happening, and that's a bit . . ."

"You're here at the worst of the year, you know, pet," said Enid cheerfully. She was putting cheese and salad on three plates, ready for dinner. "In the off-season we only get the odd little pig-rise—oh, Force 1 and 2 things—just pleasant. Just enough to keep life interesting, if you know what I mean. Oh, Bert!"

"What?"

"Did you think to open the tank?"

"Of course I did!" snapped Bert impatiently. "I'm not the one who goes to pieces in a grunter!"

"Depends what you mean by going to pieces, I'd say," said Enid tartly.

"It'll be full now, anyhow," said Bert. He went over to the side of the room and began winding a handle sticking out of the wall under the clock.

There was a creaking sound outside, and Rachel ran over to look out the window.

A big green-painted tank, like a water tank, stood next to the house. It had a lid, which was slowly closing as Bert turned his handle. As Rachel watched, the lid fitted neatly over the top of the tank and sealed it shut.

"What's in the tank?" Rachel asked Bert, her curiosity getting the better of her nervousness.

"UEF, love," Bert replied with satisfaction, giving the handle a final twist. "Force 8 at least, by the number of pigs up presently."

"But why are you keeping it?" asked Rachel, puzzled.

"Well . . . well, I mean to say, everyone does it," said Bert. "I mean, you've got to have a supply for the off-season, don't you?"

"Do you?"

Enid laughed. "'Course you do, love. What if there's no UEF for a month or two months, or something?"

"Well . . . that'd be good, wouldn't it? I mean, doesn't it make you, um, forget things, and the clock go wrong, and people disappear, and . . ."

"Oh, yes, well, that's too much of a good thing, pet. That's UEF *storms*. But what would we do without UEF at all? I mean, we've had pig-down spells—bad ones—in the past. Haven't we, Bert? Oh, dear, it's that *quiet*! No unexpected visitors, no fun on the TV, no surprises—not so much as a double-yolked egg at breakfast. You can't live like that, can you? So we always keep the tank full. We fill it usually around about now—toward the end of the season. Then, if there's a long pig-down, we can let a bit of UEF out."

"Not much, Rachel," explained Bert. "Just enough to keep us going, see, till the weather starts behaving itself. I mean, there'd never be enough to get the pigs up, even."

Rachel shook her head. How amazing. So when there was a UEF "drought" here ("pig-down," Enid called it), nothing unusual happened here at all! Ever! Maybe then . . . maybe there *was* a bit of UEF in the air at home after all. Not enough to, say, make pigs fly—but just enough to make a few unusual things happen now and then, to make life interesting.

She suddenly remembered those days when everyone at school seemed jumpy and wild for no reason. And those days when Dad complained that everyone on the road was driving crazily. And those days when you felt that excited, tingly feeling in your stomach, without knowing why. Maybe . . . maybe that was UEF. Maybe—Rachel's thoughts raced. *She'd* got here, hadn't she? Somehow or other, she'd moved from Outside to Inside. And other people had, too. Maybe the UEF leaked from Inside to Outside! Maybe, just sometimes, the world Outside got just a taste of what the people Inside lived with most of the time! When strong Inside UEF leaked out and mixed with the mild Outside UEF. . . . It was a possibility. And those funny days at home were often windy days, too. She'd noticed that. Well, well. . . .

The clock whirred, and the little pig jumped out of its house, squeaking madly. Then it stopped and stood stock-still, looking at them foolishly.

"Stupid thing!" growled Bert. "Get back inside!"

The pig didn't move. He shook his fist at it. "One of these days . . ." he growled. "How's a man supposed to know what time it is when that fool clock's always . . ."

"Turn on the TV, Bert," suggested Enid peacefully. "We might get the time off that." She grinned. "If we're lucky."

"Fat chance!" grumbled Bert. But he went over to the television set and switched it on.

There was a sharp buzzing noise, and a picture flashed onto the screen. A man in a white rabbit suit was struggling on the floor of a TV studio, hopelessly tangled up with a large rubber snake. People in headphones were running around trying to release him.

"Ah," grunted Bert in disgust. "Channel one's bitten the dust."

"What a shame," said Enid. " 'Mr. Fluff's Kids' Time,' too. Rachel might have enjoyed that."

Bert pushed a button to change channels. Channel 2 was off the air completely. On Channel 3, an ad for washing powder was running backward, very fast. A clean shirt leaped out of a smiling lady's hands, plunged into a sudsy washing machine, and flew out again with a large stain all over one sleeve. The lady looked worried and gabbled at the camera.

"Last chance," said Bert, and pushed the fourth button.

A dignified-looking newscaster with thick, wavy gray hair was sitting at a desk reading the news. On a screen behind him, a photograph of the sky cluttered with pigs was showing. The newscaster looked a little nervous, but otherwise everything seemed normal.

"Well, thank goodness for that," said Enid, and, wiping her hands on her apron, she came and stood with the others.

"The Unlikely Events Factor storm is now believed to be easing over most parts of the country," said the newscaster solemnly. "Pigs are reported to be coming down in the far west and in the north. Coastal areas are still severely affected, however, and residents are advised to continue their UEF precautions until their home pigs have dropped to window level."

"Don't have to tell us that, mate," mumbled Bert. "I wouldn't go out in that if you paid me."

"At the height of the storm," the newscaster continued smoothly, "a semitrailer on its way to the Quick-Set Dessert Company warehouse in Glenvale overturned on the bridge over Little Lake, discharging its entire load of red gelatin crystals into the water. At last report, the lake, one of the best-known tourist attractions in the Glenvale area, was still wobbly, but setting fast. It is believed that it will be solid by nightfall.

"Conservationist groups are working in relays

to release fifty ducks trapped in the gelatin. Unfortunately, the birds are resisting rescue, having developed a taste for the raspberry-flavored dessert, and several volunteers have had to receive first aid for duck-bite and severe bruising. A further nine volunteers were overcome by the UEF and are now sitting down in the lake themselves, eating dessert and refusing to move. The Police Rescue Squad has been called to the scene."

The newscaster took a deep breath, and another sheet of paper. A picture of two old ladies, identical in every way, flashed onto the screen behind him.

"On a happier note . . ." he read, "ninety-year-old Irma Strong surprised a masked burglar in the

front bedroom of her home at Crooksville this afternoon. She subdued the culprit, who was about to make off with a diamond pendant and three silver cups won by Miss Strong in local karate competitions.

"Having immobilized the burglar in a double headlock, Miss Strong removed the mask to discover that the intruder was her twin sister, Ida, whom she had not seen for eighty years.

"Miss Strong declined to press charges, and tonight the sisters are celebrating their reunion."

"There you are," said Enid comfortably. "It's an ill grunter that brings no one any good, like Mum used to say."

Rachel looked at her curiously.

"Sshh," snapped Bert. "I'm listening!"

"Twelve peanuts were injured today," said the newscaster gravely, "when the bus in which they were traveling . . ." His voice trailed off. He cleared his throat. "Sorry, I'll read that again," he said, smiling through tight lips. "Twelve people were injured today . . ."

"It's starting," said Bert glumly.

There was a crash off-camera, then a burst of jangled music and a scream. A lady in a glamorous striped dress, carrying a long pointer, lurched onto the screen in front of the news-caster's desk. Her foot seemed to be stuck in a bucket. Smiling fixedly at the camera, she lurched desperately from one side of the picture to the other, her pointer wobbling dangerously.

"It's that Sonia woman who does the weather report," said Enid in concern. "Dear, oh, dear, I hope she's careful with that pointer."

Bert snorted with laughter.

The newscaster remained in his seat, the professional smile glued to his mouth, fine beads of perspiration shining on his forehead. He read on firmly, ignoring Sonia, who was now whirling her arms wildly, trying to keep her balance.

"The . . . they were admitted to shellspital huffering from sock!" he finished triumphantly, then looked as though he wished he hadn't spoken.

With a loud scream, Sonia slipped and fell. The pointer shot from her hand like a spear, straight at the newscaster. He ducked, just in time. The pointer grazed his scalp, scooped his hair neatly from his head, and pinned it, quivering, to the screen behind him.

"It's scalped him!" screamed Enid, in horror and excitement. "Look at that! Oh!"

"It's a wig, you silly woman!" roared Bert. "It's a wig! He's bald as a badger! Look at that!"

"Good heavens, so he *is*," sighed Enid in awe. The newscaster, eyes wide with the awfulness of his situation, dropped down behind the desk and hid.

"I always *knew* his hair was too good to be true," grinned Bert, patting his own bald patch. "I might have guessed."

"Poor man," murmured Rachel, watching the newscaster stealthily crawling from behind the desk and scuttling out of the picture on all fours.

She leaned thoughtfully back in her chair. Life in a grunter certainly wasn't easy. For anyone! They were eating their salad when the clock whirred and the pig squeaked triumphantly seven times. The hands were pointing at seven o'clock. The pig retreated into its house, and the little doors snapped shut.

Bert laughed. "Looks like we're getting back to normal, love," he said to Enid. He'd been looking much happier, thought Rachel, for a while. Now he looked positively jolly. The furrow between his eyebrows had gone, and his mouth turned up instead of down.

"At last!" said Enid. "Yes—seven o'clock. Oh,

that reminds me, Bertie. Rachel'll be staying the night, of course—she can have Gloria's room. Could you climb up and get the old patchwork quilt for me?"

"Sure. Where is it?"

"Top shelf, left-hand side in the linen cupboard," Enid replied confidently. Was this the lady who couldn't even remember her husband's name a few hours ago?

There was a tapping at the window.

"Yoo-hoo, Dora, darling," bellowed Enid, waving.

A pink, piggy face, its nose pressed against the windowpane, smiled in at them. One front trotter politely tapped the glass.

"I'll go and help the old lady down, and get her to bed," said Bert. "And water the vegetables while I'm at it. You girls sit and relax. I'll do the washing up later."

"Okay, love," said Enid. She smiled at Rachel. "How would you like some chocolate ice cream, Rachel? I've just remembered I bought some yesterday. Must have known you were coming, eh?"

Rachel lay curled up in bed later that night, thinking. Gloria's life light, an ordinary-looking little lamp with a frosty glass shade, glowed comfortingly in its place by the window, and she could faintly hear Bert and Enid laughing at some TV show in the back of the house. Enid had tucked her in and given her a kiss.

"Don't fret, dearie," she'd whispered to Rachel. "Have a good, good sleep. In the morning, Bert'll take you to town. He knows the people to see. You'll be all right. We'll get you home. Just leave it to us."

I'm glad I landed on Bert and Enid's doorstep, thought Rachel drowsily. *If this had to happen, I'm glad I found them to look after me.* She resolutely kept her mind off her homesickness. *Whining won't solve anything,* she thought to herself. *That's what Dad and Mum would say. They'd say, "Be brave, Rachel, and keep your wits about you." And I will. I'll keep my wits about me, and I'll get home.* She let the warmth and softness of the bed enfold her, and her mind drift slowly into sleep.

CHAPTER 6

Mr. Len Murray of the Pilgrim's Bank

"But we have to go, we *have* to," pleaded Rachel. "We *have* to go to town. Bert, you *promised*!"

"Enid, I promised the child," said Bert anxiously. "I told her I'd take her this morning and get her some help."

"But Bertie, Rachel, my dearie, the *report*! You both heard it. They're repeating it every half hour. Force 10, they say. Probably the last one of the season, and you know what *that* means."

"A whopper, that's what it means. I know," said Bert seriously. "But this afternoon, they said, Enid. After lunch, they said. If we leave straight after breakfast . . ."

"You can't rely on *them*!" wailed Enid. "It could

come anytime, you know that, Bertie. Then where'd you be?"

"We'll be all *right*, Enid. We'll keep our eyes peeled for pigs-up and get back here like two rockets if things look dicey. You'll be okay here, love. Just keep everything shut."

Enid put her hands on her hips. "It's not me I'm worried about. It's you!" she sighed. "Both of you! But I can see it's no good trying to make you see sense. Get off with you then—quickly! Don't waste another blessed minute. And be back by lunchtime. Promise?"

"Don't worry, Mum," said Bert, swallowing his tea in a hurry. "We'll be all right, won't we, Rachel?"

Rachel nodded eagerly, cramming the last of her toast into her mouth.

"Famous last words," sniffed Enid.

She saw them to the door.

"I'm sorry I couldn't give you a dress to wear, love," she said to Rachel. "All Gloria's went years ago. And those slippers of mine don't look the best. Still—better than nothing, I suppose."

"Oh, they're good," Rachel assured her, looking with a grin at the pink fluffy scuffs on her feet. "I can hold on with my toes to keep them on, and if they flap a bit at the back it doesn't matter. It's much better than going barefoot."

"See you, love," said Bert. He gave Enid a pat and a kiss.

Rachel looked up at Enid's kind old face. The eyes weren't vague now, but smiled at her warmly. On an impulse, Rachel ran to the old lady and hugged her.

"Thank you," she said.

Enid held her tightly and kissed the top of her head. "Thank *you*, Rachel," she said.

"Cut it out, you two," laughed Bert. "No need to carry on. You'll be seeing each other again at lunchtime."

"Maybe," said Enid in a curious voice. She gave Rachel a final pat and turned her to face the door. She cleared her throat. "Well, on your way, and let me get back to work. Thanks to yesterday's effort, I've got a bit of knitting to unpick and lots of things to put straight before the grunter gets here."

She watched them from the doorway, waving, as they got into the old truck parked at the side of the house and set off along the brown dirt road. Rachel looked back as they topped the hill, and there, through a haze of dust, was Enid's white handkerchief still fluttering farewell. Then the truck went over the rise, and the house was lost to sight.

"Poor old girl," said Bert. "This has been a bit of a shock to her, you turning up." He hesitated. "Because of Gloria, see," he went on carefully.

He slowed the truck to a crawl as it passed a row of houses.

"I . . . I'm sorry," muttered Rachel. She sat back against the cracked leather seat, feeling strangely lost.

Bert leaned over and patted her shoulder. "Here, here," he said. "Come on, now. Not your fault, is it?" He broke off to wave at an old man standing at the front gate of the last house.

"That's old Jacob Simons there," he said to

Rachel. "He's wondering who you are, I bet. Loves children, Jacob does. Always had a wave for Gloria when I took her to town in the truck. He's one of the ones who saw her go, you know."

"Go?"

"Yeah. Thought Enid would've told you the story. The little one, she'd gone out looking for this kitten, see, in a grunter."

"Yes. I know—I mean, Enid told me that. But no more."

"Yeah, well—seems she was walking down the road, calling out for this blooming cat, and along come one of them big balloons with a basket underneath—the sort you can ride in, you know?"

Rachel nodded, wide-eyed. "Who was in it?" she asked.

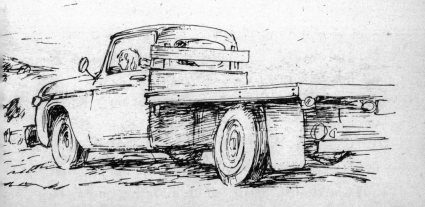

"No one, apparently," said Bert, frowning at the road ahead. "Jacob and a few other people back there saw the whole thing from their front windows. I mean, you see plenty of strange sights in a grunter, love. Unicorns in the garden, eating the lettuces as bold as you like, runaway pianos, people acting the fool. The postman got caught out in a grunter once. I'll never forget it. He ran right past our place, growling and snapping like nobody's business, chasing a pack of dogs. Bit a couple of them, too, before we could get him inside. . . ." He grinned to himself.

"Anyhow, to get back to me story," he said, "no one was really that surprised to see a loose balloon, with its basket bumping up the road, this day. But then they saw Gloria, chasing her kitten. It jumped into the basket and she followed it. And before they could do a thing about it, there was a gust of wind and the balloon was up and away. Up and away." He shook his head and pressed his lips together.

"And . . . you never found her again?" Rachel ventured.

"No. Never did," said Bert simply. "We put ads in the paper and everyone looked for her and that, but she'd just disappeared into the blue." He tapped the steering wheel thoughtfully with the tips of his fingers. "Too young to remember, see. Settled down somewhere else now."

Rachel wriggled her toes in the fluffy pink slippers and stole a look at him. He turned to smile at her.

"But that's an old story. It's your problem we're thinking about today, love. And it won't be too long now. See?" He pointed. "There's Luff's Valley, down below."

"Luff's Valley's the name of your town?" asked Rachel. "Was Luff a person?"

"Oh, too right," said Bert, slowing the truck down as they bumped across a little bridge. "Old Duckfeathers Luff was a person, all right. They named the town after him, poor old chap."

"*Duckfeathers* Luff?"

"Yep. Duckfeathers Elizabeth Luff. He came from Taunton, the next big town from here. Poor bloke. Named in a grunter, see? His mum said it seemed like a good idea at the time, so the story goes. But a name like that—phew, imagine! Half the Taunton kids called him eiderdown, and the other half called him Betty, they say. Kids can be a bit cruel like that, eh? Teasing and slinging off at him all the time, they were, and in the end he threw the whole lot in and went off and set up as a hermit here in this valley. He was on his own for years, but then a few more people moved in, and the town more or less grew up around him. He was eighty or so by that stage, though, and didn't seem to mind seeing a few people around, they say. He'd sit on the veranda of his shack, wearing a big old straw hat, with his brown dog beside him, and he'd say good day to the passersby. The women'd bring him eggs and rock cakes and jam and that. Quite a character he was. Lived to a hundred and two, old Luff did." Bert finished proudly. "And when he died they pulled down the shack and built the town hall on the land, with a brass plate telling all about him."

The truck rattled cautiously past a DANGER PIGS CROSSING sign, and into the main street of Luff's Valley.

"Now," said Bert, "first thing, we're going to the bank to see Len Murray, the manager. He had an Outsider working for him for a while. It was ten years ago, but I reckon he'll remember something about it. He was fit to be tied when the bloke left without warning. Had the whole place upside down checking no money'd gone with him."

"Had it?" asked Rachel eagerly.

"Nup. 'Course not. I met the bloke myself a couple of times. He wasn't the type. Nice chap he was. Always ready with a joke. But he did up and disappear very suddenly, see? And Len's a cautious sort of chap."

Bert swung the truck into a parking space outside a small stone building. One of the columns on either side of its solid-looking door carried a dignified brass plate. PILGRIM'S BANK—LUFF'S VALLEY BRANCH it announced. The door was firmly closed.

"We'll go around the side, Rachel," said Bert. "Len said to. I spoke to him on the phone last night. Bank doesn't open for an hour, yet."

Rachel scrambled out of the truck and shuffled quickly onto the pavement in her floppy slippers. Bert clambered from his place, climbed down to the road, and joined her.

"Right," he said, hitching at his belt. "Let's see how we go."

Rachel shuffled along beside him as he made his way slowly down the lane beside the bank, toward a white door in the side of the building. Her heart was beating fast. Surely, surely a clever and important man like Mr. Len Murray, manager of the Luff's Valley branch of the Pilgrim's Bank, would give her the clue she needed to find her way home.

Bert knocked at the door and they waited. Footsteps approached slowly.

Hurry up, hurry up, Mr. Murray, thought Rachel, in an agony of impatience.

The locks drew back inside and the door opened.

Rachel screamed.

A monstrous gray face loomed out at them, its blank eyes shining like a huge fly's. A hand stretched out and grabbed Rachel's arm.

"Come in," boomed a hollow voice. "Quickly. Come in!"

". . . So you see, Rachel, Mr. Murray always wears a gas mask in a grunter, to protect him from

the UEF. See? I should've warned you, only I didn't think he'd have it on yet. Grunter's not predicted till after lunch, Len."

The masked face behind the desk nodded.

"Can't be too careful, Bert," said the muffled voice.

Rachel stared at the apparition with round eyes. The contrast between Mr. Murray's portly figure in its neat gray suit and tie, the soft, plump hands with their gold watch and wedding ring folded calmly on the polished desk top, and the grotesque gray rubber face, with its hoselike nose and plastic eye windows, was horrible. She still shivered a little with the fright she had had at the door.

"Would it be possible, d'you reckon, Len, to take the mask off just while we're talking? Skies are clear, mate. Not a sign of pigs-up, yet," said Bert persuasively.

"Well," said the hollow voice, "maybe just for ten minutes."

Mr. Murray fumbled with the straps of his gas mask and pulled it off. He sat blinking at them—a plump, pink-cheeked man with a clipped brown mustache and a shiny bald head haloed with a fluff of brown hair. He self-consciously smoothed the fluff into a tidy fringe.

"Now, then," he said, in a fussy clipped voice very different from the hollow, terrifying boom that had reached them through the mask, "how can I help you?"

"I explained our situation on the phone last night, Len. Rachel here's an Outsider, and she's keen to get back home as fast as she can. I said I'd help her. You're someone who's had experience with Outsiders, and . . ."

"With one Outsider, yes," interrupted the bank manager, adjusting a small pile of papers on his tidy desk with his fingertips. "But I don't know, Bert, as I told you, where he went when he left here, or how he left. All I know is that he went, suddenly, without a breath of warning, in the middle of a Force 10 grunter—the worst possible time for us, as you can imagine." He had flushed a little and sounded rather indignant.

"He went out for his lunch break, before the grunter began, and never returned. And I had to lock up and cope with the staff by myself, as best I could. It was most inconvenient. Young Angela Perkins locked herself in the safe and ate several bills and four coins before we could get her out. Then twelve dozen boxes of chocolate teddy bears fell off a truck just outside the main door and blocked it completely. And the computer took it into its head to send extra interest payments to any customer who was born in a month with an 'R' in its name. The usual sort of thing, Bert, but I'd grown to depend on Alexander. As an Outsider, of course, he was unaffected by the UEF. He was valuable to me. And of course he'd been a bank teller Outside. Their ways of doing things are quite similar to ours, apparently. That was why I took him on in the first place."

"He was a reliable sort of chap, then, Len, in your view?" asked Bert thoughtfully.

"Oh, yes. A very diligent worker. A bit dreamy now and then, I must say—not, I would say, a banker by *nature*, you understand, Bert, but on the whole a reliable, diligent worker. The only time I ever had to speak to him severely was over paper wastage. He was forever filling his pads up with bits of notes about Outsiders—the silliest things, sometimes. And in meetings he'd doodle and draw all over his notes. I don't like waste—or untidiness—in my bank. So I spoke to him about it, and he saw my point of view straight away."

"The notes were probably because he was trying to find his way home—like me," said Rachel in a small voice.

"Very probably, Rachel," said Mr. Murray kindly. "Very probably. I didn't say he shouldn't take notes at all, dear. I simply said he should make them in his own time—at lunchtime or in the evening. And on his own personal note-paper."

He looked at his watch and picked up his gas mask.

"I'm very sorry that I haven't been able to offer any real advice, Bert," he said, rising from his chair and holding out his hand. "Mrs. Titterton in Noddy's Lane was Alexander's landlady, as you know. Perhaps she can give you some more information. I'll ring and let her know you're on your way."

Bert shook hands with him and glanced at Rachel. Mr. Murray obviously wanted to get back to his work, and there was no point in arguing with him.

At the door, Mr. Murray smiled in a friendly way at Rachel.

"Once you're settled, Rachel, pop in and see us. You can't start saving too early, you know. Children under fourteen receive a Happy Pilgrim Money Box free when they start an account with us."

"Thank you," whispered Rachel, and the white door shut, leaving her standing with Bert in the lane.

"He thinks I'll never get home!" she said, and bit her lip.

"Don't worry, love. He's a bit of a stick-in-the-mud, Len is. We'll go and visit Cathy Titterton now, and see what she has to tell us. We can walk in from here, easy. Noddy's Lane's just around the corner."

CHAPTER 7
The Amazing Cathy Titterton

Rachel shuffle-trotted along beside Bert, thinking carefully. Actually, they had learned a few things from Mr. Murray. They'd learned that his Outsider had been keeping notes about other Outsiders, so probably he was trying to find his way home, just like she was. He was a reliable sort of man, yet he left suddenly, without giving Mr. Murray any warning. That probably meant that he found the way home suddenly. He was given a chance and he had to take it, then and there.

"And it happened at lunchtime!" said Rachel aloud.

"What?" Bert looked at her in surprise.

"Nothing. I was just working something out. Mr. Murray's Outsider left suddenly, at lunchtime. We have to find out what he was doing during the lunch break on that day."

"Eating lunch, I suppose," said Bert, shrugging his shoulders.

"But *where*?" insisted Rachel. "That's the important thing." A thought struck her. "Or *what*! Maybe what he *ate* is the answer."

"Here's Mrs. Titterton's place. Maybe she'll know," said Bert, stopping at a house with a yellow door and a doormat to match.

"Will she be wearing a gas mask, too?" asked Rachel nervously.

Bert sniggered. "Not likely. The madder things are, the better Cathy Titterton likes it, so I hear."

He rang a little bell attached to the doorknob.

"Coming!" sang a high voice.

The door was flung wide, and a tall, thin, smiling lady with huge eyes and a beaky nose held out her arms in welcome. The great sleeves of the scarlet robe she was wearing waved like wings and shimmered in the sunlight.

"Hello, hello—please come in. Mr. Murray said you'd call."

She ushered them into a sitting room in the

front of the house. It was filled with pictures, or-naments, statues, and dried-flower arrangements. Over every chair a different-colored cloth or shawl was draped. There was a bright blue rug on the floor. Pink pigs sailed around its border in a com-plicated pattern.

"Sit down, and tell me all about it, darlings," said Cathy Titterton, perching on the edge of a couch like some exotic bird.

Bert lowered himself into the least dangerous-looking chair and then leaped up again. A bundle of fur that he had taken for a cushion meowed crossly and jumped onto the floor, shaking its head. It looked back at him in fury and began lick-ing its tousled fur with a bright pink tongue.

Bert looked hunted.

"Sorry," he said. He sat down again, cleared his throat, and jingled the truck keys in his pocket. He obviously felt uncomfortable in this strange lady's house.

"Aah . . ." he began, and smoothed his gray hair nervously.

"We came to ask," said Rachel firmly, "about the Outsider who used to live in this house."

"Alex? Ah!" Mrs. Titterton lifted her arms and waggled her long fingers. The scarlet sleeves dropped back to her elbows in luxurious folds, and Bert mumbled nervously to himself.

"Alex was just a sweetie! That's the only word for Alex. A real sweetie. A lovely person. Always joking, never a cross word. The nicest boarder I ever had. Of course, I have an affinity with Librans." She leaned forward and smiled at Rachel.

"What's your sign, darling?"

"Um . . . Aries," murmured Rachel.

"Ah . . . the Ram—very determined. I suppose that's why you've wasted no time seeing about getting home. Alex wasn't so fussed. More relaxed at first. Of course, later on he did get a bit pippy, poor dear boy, and he did start trying to get back home, and I must say once he'd set his mind to it he worked away at it like mad. Oh, I used to say to him, oh, I only wish *I* was so organized. But, of course, I'm Pisces, the artistic type, you see, and we're so . . ." She turned to Bert abruptly.

"What about you, sweetie," she said. "What's your sign?"

Bert's face slowly reddened. "Haven't got a clue," he said gruffly.

"Oh, let me guess, then—oh, Taurus, that's it! I just bet you're a Taurean. The strong, silent, masculine type!" She wiggled her bony fingers at him.

Rachel saw with wonder that each long nail was painted a different color.

"The thing is, ah, Mrs. Titterton," said Bert determinedly, "we were hoping you could tell us a bit about—ah—Alex."

"About the day he left, especially," added Rachel, leaning forward. "What he ate, and everything."

"What he *ate*?" Cathy Titterton gave a silvery laugh. "My dear, I couldn't possibly remember

that! It was nearly ten years ago! I can't even remember what *I* ate *yesterday*!"

Rachel felt desperate. "Couldn't you try?" she begged. Mrs. Titterton waggled her fingers, smiled, and shrugged her shoulders in a daffy, helpless sort of way.

Then Rachel had an inspiration. "Couldn't you," she said as dramatically as she could, "cast yourself back in time and . . . and relive that day ten years ago?"

"Oh . . ." Mrs. Titterton began to look interested. "Put myself into a trance, you mean, and travel back across the years?"

"Well . . . sort of," said Rachel uncertainly.

"Ah . . . what fun!" cried Cathy Titterton. "I'll try."

She threw her head back and closed her eyes. She began slowly rocking from side to side, breathing deeply.

Bert raised his eyebrows at Rachel, who raised her eyebrows back and shrugged. They waited a full minute. Bert's stomach rumbled noisily. He patted it and glanced nervously at his watch; Rachel clenched her fists till her nails stuck into her palms. Any minute Bert would say they had to go, and then—

"It's coming to me . . . yes . . ." said Mrs. Titterton in a dreamy voice, without opening her eyes. "It's coming. Alex . . . I recall it as clearly as if it were yesterday. Alex, Mrs. Simkiss, Mr. Sneed—my three boarders—all sitting at breakfast, talking . . . talking about the grunter coming. Yes. They were eating . . . sausages! I remember because Tiddles, naughty cattikins, had stolen one and I'd burned one of the others, so we only had half a one each. It must have been a Thursday. We always had sausages on Thursday. . . ."

Her voice trailed off. They waited, and at last she began to speak again.

"Mr. Sneed said he'd be going back to bed. He always did when a Force 10 was predicted, dear old chap. I said to him, he missed so much! But he said that was the whole idea!" Mrs. Titterton's eyes opened wide. "I can't understand people like that, can you?" she exclaimed to Bert.

"Well . . ." Bert mumbled.

"Oh—I *adore* a good grunter. I always leave the windows wide open so I can get the full benefit. You can't *imagine* the amazing things that have happened in this house, darling. You just can't *imagine!*"

"I've got a fair idea," said Bert stolidly.

Rachel could well understand why Mr. Sneed stayed in bed on a Force 10 day. Cathy Titterton was amazing enough on a normal day without the added amazements of UEF flooding the house.

"So," Cathy went on, "Mr. Sneed went back upstairs. Alex and Mrs. Simkiss went to work. They took a packed lunch—cheese and pickle sandwiches, it was. . . ."

"Oh, are you sure?" exclaimed Rachel excitedly.

"Absolutely *positive*, darling!" cried Cathy triumphantly. "I've cast myself back and I can just *see* it!"

"Oh, Bert!" Rachel turned to Bert with a glowing face, but he held up his hand gently.

"Ah—what did they usually take for lunch, then," he asked casually.

"Oh—ah—well, cheese and pickle sandwiches, actually," said Cathy, a little crushed.

"Oh, no!" groaned Rachel, bitterly disappointed. "But that means—oh—that means that what he ate for lunch that day had nothing to do with why he suddenly disappeared. I mean, if he had the same thing *every* day. . . ."

"Well, it was his own fault," said Cathy defensively. "I don't think Alex noticed what he ate, really, in those last few months. He'd just bolt his lunch down in the park and go over to the library, to make those endless notes. I mean, darling, I was always offering different, yummy things— curried banana, peanut butter and sardines, pickled liver and beetroot—yummy, *original* fillings. But he was such a stick-in-the-mud, like all the others." She sighed. "He'd just say, 'Oh, please, Cathy, just the usual will be fine!'" She sighed again. "They didn't know what they were missing."

"Er—yes—" said Bert, looking a bit sick. He got to his feet. "Well," he said to Rachel, looking curiously at her suddenly shining eyes, "we'd better be going, love. It's nearly lunchtime." He turned to Cathy. "Force 10 coming up, you know," he said.

"I *know*," squealed Cathy, clasping her hands. "Isn't it *wonderful!*"

"Er—yes . . ." Bert backed toward the door. He tripped over the cat. "Oh, sorry," he muttered. "Well, thanks for . . ."

"Oh, I've got a marvelous idea!" exclaimed Cathy. "Why don't you stay for lunch and watch pig-rise with me, darlings? I'll make a plate of sandwiches—really yummy, *original* sandwiches, and we'll . . ."

"Oh, look, thanks very much, Mrs. Titterton," mumbled Bert, backing away even faster. "But we've just got to go, haven't we, Rachel?"

He found the door and opened it.

"Thanks again," he gabbled, and bundled Rachel into the street.

"Another time, then," trilled Cathy, waving from the door.

"Have a nice grunter," called Rachel, waving back.

"I will. Same to you! Bye!"

Cathy was still waving as they turned the corner.

"Phew!" breathed Bert. "What a terrible woman! I'm glad I don't live with her. Force 10 nightmare, that'd be. Useless visit, too, love. Sorry. We didn't get a thing out of it."

"But Bert, we *did*, we *did*," laughed Rachel, capering around him in her flip-floppy slippers. "We found out that Alex always went to the *library* at lunchtime. The *library*! He disappeared at lunchtime. But it wasn't because of what he ate! It was because of something that happened at the library!"

Bert looked at her and smoothed his bald patch thoughtfully.

"You might be on to something there," he said. He checked his watch. "We've still got time," he said, "if we hurry. Library's on the main street, just near the bank. Let's get going!"

CHAPTER 8
Pigs Are Up!

Rachel and Bert hurried up Luff's Row, the main street of the little town. It was full of people bustling around buying last-minute supplies so that they wouldn't have to go out in the grunter.

"The library's just ahead," puffed Bert.

They edged through a long queue of people snaking across the footpath in front of them.

"What are they all waiting for?" asked Rachel curiously, looking back.

"Lottery tickets!" snorted Bert. "There's always a rush just before a big grunter. High UEF, see. People think to themselves, 'What's more unlikely than that I'll win the lottery? Quick, I'd better buy a ticket!' So they all rush off and jam the lottery office. Half of them'll end up caught in the grunter, for sure. Silly fools! Only one person can win it, same as always. Isn't that right?"

"I guess so," said Rachel.

"'Course," Bert went on reflectively, "there was that time they printed the tickets in a grunter— oh, five or six years ago. That time everyone won."

"Everyone?"

"Yeah—all the tickets had the same number on them, see? Some machine error, they said, and they refused to pay—sent all the winners a free lottery ticket instead of the money. Yes—five or six years ago that was. The Great Luff's Valley Lottery Riot. Took them six months to rebuild the old lottery office—just a big pile of bricks it was, by the time those disappointed winners had finished with it. The staff'd gone up a big tree at the back when the front doors went. Fire rescue blokes had to get them down in the end." He laughed. "They never print lottery tickets in a grunter now," he said.

They climbed the library steps and went through the swinging glass door into cool silence.

A stocky, gray-haired woman was checking cards at the front desk.

"We're in luck," whispered Bert. "That's Connie Coolie—been here for donkey's years. She'll remember your Outsider if he came in here a lot."

They approached the desk, Bert's shoes squeaking and Rachel's slippers flapping, on the smooth vinyl-covered floor.

"Connie," said Bert in a low voice. The woman looked up.

"Yes? Ah—Bert. Hello." She smiled.

"This is Rachel. Rachel, Miss Coolie. Connie, Rachel's an Outsider, and she . . ."

Bert went into their story once more and Rachel, feeling Miss Coolie's sympathetic eyes on her, withdrew for a moment into a little world of her own. The truth was, no place she'd been in so far in her extraordinary adventure had so reminded her of home. This was just like her own local library. It smelled the same. The orderly rows of bookshelves, the comfortable chairs, the posters about books and reading—they all looked the same. A sickening wave of homesickness rose up and almost washed her away into a flood of tears. She fought it back.

Don't give up now, you silly thing, she said to herself. *Be brave—that's what Mum'd say. Keep your wits about you—that's what Dad would say.*

She made her mouth into a firm, straight line

and put her shoulders back. She tuned in to what
Miss Coolie was saying.

"Of course. I remember perfectly, Bert. Every
day he'd come, poor man. Every day at lunchtime
for six months or so. He worked his way through
the whole library, more or less. Took masses of
notes, and they never seemed to get him anywhere. But he never gave up." She shook her

head. "And I must say he never looked all that downhearted, while he was here. He was always ready for a joke. The people at Mr. Murray's bank aren't encouraged to joke very much, I don't think. I think, perhaps," she cleared her throat, "that Alexander wasn't really—er—cut out to be a bank teller. But that's what he'd trained for, he said, as a lad, and he'd never, he said, felt confident enough to make a change. Rather sad, really. But"—she raised her eyebrows and smiled—"he always said that if he ever got home, things would be different. I've often wondered if they were. . . ."

"Then you think he got home—that he got back Outside?" cried Rachel eagerly, forgetting to speak softly.

"I'm sure he did, dear. I'm just certain of it. And I'll tell you why.

"He was sitting here reading as usual and taking notes—he was on to the end of the children's section by then, down here in the corner. He was in fairly good spirits. He told me that from what he'd been able to find out, Outsiders who lived near schools seemed to disappear more quickly than Outsiders who didn't. So he was looking at the children's books very carefully.

"We were doing the windows and closing the ventilators and so on because of the grunter—Force 10 predicted that day, Bert. There was no one but Alexander and the staff here. Everyone else had gone back to work or gone home, but, being an Outsider, he didn't have to worry about getting back before pig-rise.

"Well—Alexander was sitting quietly there, reading, and all of a sudden he jumped up and sort of—well, really, he yelled! Shouted out. We all nearly jumped out of our skins! I'll never forget it. He started jumping around and dropped the book he'd been reading. He saw me watching him and rushed up and"—she flushed slightly—"gave me a great big hug and a kiss. And he yelled, 'I've got it, Connie!' He was so excited! 'I'm going home!' he said. 'Out of the mouths of babes!'

"I said, 'Alexander, what is it?' or 'What do you mean?' or something like that. 'You'd better get back to the bank. The town hall pig's up,' I said, because I could see it through the window. It was always first to go in those days, being just a piglet really. Their old one had just died. 'Mr. Murray will be needing you quite soon, Alexander,' I said.

"'Oh, no!' he yelled, right in my ear. I was nearly deafened. He let go of me and sort of looked wildly all around. Then he ran to the desk, put down some money, and grabbed my new thermos flask—the one I had my coffee in, for lunch.

" 'Sorry, Connie,' he said. 'Buy a new one on me—no time to explain. Thanks for everything,' he said. And then he just flew out those front doors, and I never saw him again." She smiled and shook her head. "I'm certain he got home, though. Somehow I just *know* it. He must have needed my thermos so he'd have something to drink on the way. It must have been a long trip."

"But—" exploded Rachel, "but Miss Coolie— which book was he reading? Is it still here?"

"Well, there were several books on his chair. Four of them, actually, and I don't know which one he was reading when he left . . . but, dear, they were only little children's books. They couldn't have had anything to do with . . ."

"Oh, *please*," pleaded Rachel. "*Please!* One of them *must* have something. Some clue. Can you think of their names?"

"Well, of course I can. I looked at them particularly. They were *Suki the Brave Dog* . . ."

"We've got that at home," said Bert proudly.

"Yes, well, it's a classic, isn't it, Bert . . . then there was *Alfie the Ant*, a picture book, and its companion *Rosalie the Rat*—silly books, both of them. I've never liked them but some children do, so they stay on the shelves, of course. And—now—what was the fourth book? Goodness gracious me, my poor head. . . ." She wrinkled her nose and tapped her sleek gray head in irritation.

"Look," she said, taking Rachel's hand over the counter. "I'll get those three for you, anyway, and you can start looking at them, and I'll have another think while I'm doing the windows." She glanced at Bert.

"What are your plans for the grunter, Bert?"

"We're supposed to get home before it starts!" said Bert nervously.

"You're cutting it a bit fine, aren't you?" said Connie Coolie, eyebrows raised.

A young man ran, catlike, down the stairs beside the desk.

"Pigs up yet, John?" she asked him.

"No, Connie, not that I can see. Can't be far off it now, though." The man looked curiously at Bert and Rachel and walked soundlessly off to the back

of the library. They heard him rattling each window as he checked it.

"It's very important to the girl, Connie," said
Bert gravely.

Connie Coolie stepped smartly out from behind the desk and led Rachel to the children's section of the library. She scanned one shelf and
pulled three books down. She put them on a
table.

"Here you are, dear," she said quietly. "Go for
your life. Now—none of the other books on that
shelf ring a bell. It's possible that the fourth book's
in the basement for binding repairs. I'll pop down
and check the rebinds now—there aren't too
many. If I find it I'll send my assistant up with
it. Excuse me not coming myself but I really have
to make sure everything's secure. A Force 10's
appalling in a library, as you can imagine!"
She smiled at Rachel, waved to Bert, and scur-
ried back to the desk and down some stairs behind it.

Rachel sat down at the table and began to scan
the books. She looked at *Alfie the Ant* first. She
knew she didn't have much time, and her finger
was trembling as she ran it over the lines of big,
clear type, trying not to miss anything important.

Bert leaned on the desk, watching her. He ran his hand over his bald patch and cleared his throat.

"Rachel," he said. "Love, I'm going to pop over the road to the hardware shop. Their pig had a litter a couple of months ago, and they kept one of the piglets. It'll be the first to go. The smaller they are, see, the faster they rise. Now, I'm going to watch that little pig and when it goes, we've got to go, too, see, Rachel? That's cutting it as fine as we possibly can. As soon as its fat little trotters leave the ground, I'm going to rush across the road, get in the truck, and toot for you. You've got to promise me, love, that you'll come the instant you hear that horn. Now, do you promise?"

"Yes, Bert, I promise," said Rachel, her eyes glued to the book. She felt the old man's eyes on her and looked up. "I do promise, really and truly. I'll come as soon as you toot," she said earnestly. "Don't worry."

"Okay, then," said Bert. "I'll be waiting for you."

He turned and walked slowly out of the library, only glancing back once.

Rachel nodded vigorously at him, and he waved and disappeared down the stairs.

*   *   *

Alfie the Ant was a boring story about an ant who kept disobeying his mother and getting into trouble. It seemed to hold no clues of any kind. Rachel put it aside and picked up *Rosalie the Rat*. It was just as boring and just as unhelpful. With a sinking heart, Rachel began flipping through the pages of *Suki the Brave Dog*. It was a long book—a proper novel. She knew she couldn't read every line in the time she had. She feverishly ran her finger down each page, trying to take in the story. She grew hotter and hotter, and could feel her hands getting slippery with perspiration.

"Suki grabbed Pete's shirt in her strong little teeth and pulled with all her might . . ." she read. Oh, heavens, how could she know what was important and what wasn't? How big or how tiny was the clue that had made that man called Alexander suddenly jump up shouting, knowing he'd found his way home?

Soft footsteps squeaked behind her chair and she looked up.

A fair young woman with kind brown eyes smiled down at her. "Rachel, I'm Miss Rider," she said, holding out a book. "Miss Coolie said you wanted this."

Rachel grabbed at the book eagerly.

"Oh, careful," said Miss Rider. "The back cover's come away from the binding. It's an old book, out of print now, and quite valuable. We want to repair it and put it back on the shelves."

"Sorry," whispered Rachel, and put the book carefully in her lap. She looked at the faded title and her heart sank.

Child's Play: Skipping Rhymes and Playground Chants.

"That can't be it," she said, and the tears finally came into her eyes and rolled down her cheeks.

"Oh, come on, chin up," said Miss Rider, bending over her. "Don't be disappointed, Rachel. Miss Coolie told me about you, and I know you must feel awful—but this is your first day looking, isn't it? You can try again tomorrow, or the next day."

Rachel shook her head. "I'll never, never do it," she sobbed. "I'm not big enough or old enough. I can't work it out."

"You will," said Miss Rider. "We'll help you, Rachel, honestly . . . goodness, what on earth . . . can you hear that car horn? It's been going for ages. I wonder what . . ."

Rachel's stomach leaped with a sickening thud.

"Pigs are up!" called the young man, running for the stairs.

"It's Bert! Oh, I didn't hear him. Oh, I promised I'd come straight away!" Rachel ran for the library door, the old book clutched in her hand.

"Hold on!" cried Miss Rider. "Rachel, wait! Stop!"

"I can't! I promised!"

CHAPTER 9
It's Got Her!

Rachel stumbled down the stairs and made for the truck. Bert was leaning on the horn, revving the engine.

"Hurry up!" he roared. "They're all going up! Hurry!"

Rachel wrenched open the door and leaped into the passenger seat beside him. "Bert, I'm sorry . . ." she began.

"Snakes alive!" exploded Bert. "Where've you been? I've been . . . Rachel, who's that woman?"

Rachel looked out the window and was amazed to see Miss Rider running toward them, calling and waving her arms.

Suddenly she realized what was wrong.

"Oh! Oh! I forgot to leave the book. It's valu-able—she said—oh, dear, oh, Bert. . . ."

Bert ground his teeth in frustration.

"Give it back to her, quick!" he snapped. "We've got to get going!"

Rachel opened the door just as Miss Rider, hair flying, reached the truck.

"I'm so sorry," gasped Rachel, thrusting the book toward her. "I didn't think!"

"Oh, thank goodness I caught you!" panted Miss Rider. "I've only been at this library a week, and if Miss Coolie . . ." Suddenly she stopped. A curious expression came over her face. She sniffed and blinked. "That's . . . funny," she said. "I . . ."

"Get back into the library, miss!" barked Bert, peering in despair through the windscreen at the road ahead. "Pigs are up all over the place!"

Miss Rider rubbed the back of her hand over her forehead and shook her head. Her gentle brown eyes were bewildered.

"Something . . ." she said dreamily.

"Quick!" bawled Bert. "Shut the door, Rachel."

"No, wait!" shouted Miss Rider. "Let me in! I'm coming with you."

"Oh, no," groaned poor Bert, burying his face in his hands. "It's got her! Oh, glory! What'll Connie Coolie say—"

"Rachel, move over!" begged Miss Rider. "Make room."

Dumbfounded, Rachel slid across the seat, and the librarian leaped into the truck beside her. She slammed the door, and Bert took off, with a screech of tires. He hunched over the wheel, his knuckles white.

The truck pounded up the deserted street and out of the town.

Rachel stole a look at the woman sitting beside her. She was still panting, and her cheeks were flushed. Her hair had come down and was hanging on her shoulders. Miss Rider looked around and saw her staring.

"I had to come," she said apologetically.

"Why?" said Rachel.

"Um—I don't know," said Miss Rider helplessly.

Bert snorted.

Up ahead, a bell began to clang furiously.

"Hopeless!" exploded Bert. "Hopeless blithering idiots!"

"What is it?" gasped Rachel, craning to see.

"The blooming fire station's on fire again!" said Bert in disgust. "There—see?"

Sure enough, smoke was billowing from the up-stairs windows of the fire station. A dozen fire fighters, in all stages of undress, were battling the blaze. Their captain, wearing flowered shorts, boots, and a shiny helmet, danced around shout-ing orders through a megaphone. As the truck shot past, he turned away and pretended to be examining something behind him on the ground.

"Embarrassed!" snorted Bert. "And so he should be. Have you ever? Every blooming season that place burns down! Wouldn't credit it, would you?"

Rachel shook her head, eyes wide.

By the roadside, groups of grown-up pigs had gathered, grunting with excitement as their piglets tumbled above them. Some of the more slender adults already floated just off the ground. Their ears waved in the breeze as the truck roared past them.

Rachel leaned back against the seat and began flipping the pages of the book that had caused so much trouble. Some of the playground rhymes seemed vaguely familiar. She read a verse aloud.

Piggsy Wiggsy
Sat in her sty.
Piggsy Wiggsy
Started to cry.
Then came a grunter
UEF 10—
Piggsy Wiggsy
Happy again!

She looked out at the pigs—yes, they loved it, all right. Funny how old rhymes that seemed nonsense often said true things. Like nursery rhymes at home—all about kings and queens and things that happened long ago. They'd been around so long, those rhymes, that people had forgotten they had serious meanings. They were just fun to sing and chant. No one took notice of what the words really meant.

She caught Miss Rider's eye.

"I wish I would be happy again," she said, trying to smile.

"You'll be okay, Rachel," said Bert, passing a sedately trotting zebra wearing a party hat. "We'll get you home in the end."

"But how long will it take?"

"Sure, it could take a while," said Miss Rider,

taking her hand. "But you'll make it. You know, I lost my home when I was a little girl, too. And I never did find my way back. That's because here it happens all the time, and I forgot who I belonged to, and where I came from. It happens to lots of people. But you're different. You're an Outsider. You remember, and you'll get back because of that. Won't she, Mr. . . . um? . . ."

"Bert," said the old man briefly. "Bert Beddoes. Yeah. They all get back, somehow or other, if they want to enough. I've told her that."

The librarian looked at him carefully, and her forehead wrinkled slightly.

"What happened to you?" asked Rachel.

"Well—it was a day just like today, they told me, and . . . oh! Look out!"

A plane swooped crazily overhead, just clearing the treetops. As they watched, a box fell from the plane and burst on the roadway in front of them. Thousands of Ping-Pong balls flew from the box and bounced off in all directions.

Bert feverishly swerved the truck and miraculously missed the wreckage.

"Mad fool!" he shouted, shaking his fist at the plane. "Flying in a grunter—he'll lose his license for sure, if he's not killed. Oh, glory—I'm mad myself, driving in this weather. If we get home in one piece, I'll be a pig's dinner!"

Rachel caught the librarian looking at Bert with that same curious expression.

"Bert gets a bit cranky, in grunters," she murmured defensively.

"Oh, yes . . ." said Miss Rider. "I was just . . ."

"Tell me the rest about when you lost your home," said Rachel quickly.

"Oh, there's nothing much to tell," said Miss Rider, holding on tightly as the truck lurched on the dusty road. "I was only little—five years old, apparently—and I turned up on a dear old lady's doorstep in the middle of a grunter with a black kitten in my arms. No clues about where I'd come from. Nothing at all—except this little brooch, see?" She showed Rachel a little brooch pinned to her collar.

"A little gold pig—oh, isn't it sweet!" said Rachel, touching it with the tip of her finger.

She felt Bert give a little jump beside her. She looked up. They'd nearly reached the crest of the hill. Soon the white house would be in view. Enid would be waiting. On the green slopes beside the road, some big pigs were clustered, nuzzling each other. Above them, their smaller brothers and sisters dipped and swung.

"I always wear it, this little brooch," said Miss Rider dreamily. "One day, one piggy day, I know I'm going to find my old home again, and the people who loved me, and they'll see the brooch, and they'll know. . . ."

Bert spoke gruffly. "Was the old lady a good sort?" he said. "Treat you well, and that?"

"Oh, she was lovely. Auntie Rose, I used to call her. She looked after me as if I was her own. I could only remember my first name, so I took her last name. Her name was Rose Rider. But I always wondered—always, even before Auntie Rose died—about the family I'd come from. I had these nice memories. . . ."

"What memories," said Bert, even more gruffly.

"Oh, you know, being tucked up under a patchwork quilt, being kissed good night by someone with soft skin, a big white room, the smell of lavender, a funny clock on the wall . . . you know, the things a five-year-old would remember." Miss Rider sighed. "After Auntie Rose died, I was so lonely and lost. I felt I'd lost a family twice, I suppose. That's really why I moved here. I felt restless and when I saw the job advertised, right across on the other side of the country, I thought—'Well, why not?' I don't know. I just felt it was time to see this part of the world. I saw the ad in a grunter, needless to say." She laughed.

The truck topped the rise.

"Oh, look at that lovely little house down there," said Miss Rider.

"That's ours," said Bert in a curious voice.

"It's lovely. . . ." The librarian rubbed her forehead again. "I . . . it must be the grunter, you know. I really feel so . . . that house looks so . . . I mean, I'm sorry I jumped into your truck like that. It was the smell of the leather, I think. It seemed so familiar. And now this house! You must think I'm . . ."

"You'd be twenty-five now, then, would you, love?" asked Bert, carefully not looking at her.

She stared at him in surprise. "How do you know that?" she asked.

With beating heart, Rachel looked from one to the other as the truck bounced toward the little white house. She faced the front and gripped the seat. In the sky, the pigs were tumbling and massing. Just a few of the fattest were still grounded on the green hill. And straight ahead was the house. Rachel stared at it in wonder. A glow was rising in one of the front windows. Was it fire? No—not like a fire. It didn't flicker. It was strong, like a beacon, and pulsing like a heartbeat.

"Bert!" She pointed.

He looked, and for a moment his firm old chin trembled.

"It's the life light in the bedroom window!" cried Rachel. "It's . . ."

"She always said it, the old girl," said Bert, almost to himself. " 'One piggy day,' she said. She never doubted it for a minute, no matter what I said or how I argued. And she was right, true old heart. Right all along."

"I'm sorry," said the librarian, bewildered. "That light . . . I don't . . ."

"It's your life light, welcoming you home, Gloria," said Bert, and the truck thundered to a stop outside the house, shining now in every window with the life-light glow.

The door flew open, and Enid was there, eyes wide, hand over her mouth.

"She knows," breathed Rachel in awe. "The life light told her you were coming. She's waiting for you. Oh—oh, Miss Rider—Gloria—hurry! . . ."

But Gloria was already out of the door and rushing into Enid's arms.

Outsider Inside

"Got to get them inside," puffed Bert, wrestling with his own door handle. "Must be UEF 8 already, and you know how Enid gets—but, oh, dear, she's not going to forget much today, Force 10 or no Force 10. Gloria's one thing that's never slipped her mind. Mine, neither, for that matter. I bought her that little piglet brooch myself." He jumped from the truck.

"Come on, love," he called to Rachel, over the rising wind. "Come in and celebrate with us. It's all because of you this's happened. All because of you and that blessed old book!" He made for the house. "Come on!" he bellowed from the doorway.

"In a minute!" Rachel shouted back. "UEF

doesn't worry me. Shut the door! I'll knock!"

He raised a hand in farewell, and disappeared into the house.

Rachel sat quietly for a moment, her hands clasped in her lap. So Gloria was home. The grunter had brought her back, against all odds. Back into town from across the country, to the library where Bert so often went, to the truck, because of a forgetful little girl, into the truck because of a remembered childhood smell, and home to the little white house in the valley, and an old woman who'd waited for her for twenty years.

Rachel's eyes swam with tears. She had a home, where her mother's feet clattered up and down the stairs and her father whistled in the bath, where Jamie cooed to himself in bed at night and the next-door cat slept on a warm brick wall in the garden. And where was her home now? And all the people *she* loved?

Almost without meaning to, she picked up the battered old book and flipped the pages. The nonsense rhymes and chants, so like the ones she skipped and clapped to at school, swam through her tears on the thick yellow pages.

She'd tried so hard to be brave. She'd tried hard

to keep her wits about her. She flipped the pages. Kids' rhymes. Nonsense rhymes. . . . Outsiders who lived near schools got home faster, Alexander had said. . . . He'd shouted, "Out of the mouths of babes!" and he'd jumped . . .

Rachel stared at the page before her and furiously rubbed the tears from her eyes.

One of the oldest recorded skipping rhymes said the note at the top of the page. *Its origins are lost in time, but children are still using it today, in hundreds of different versions. Here is one of the oldest:*

The beat of the verse was the same as all of those she'd chanted herself. You could see the children turning the rope, the children jumping, their feet sending up puffs of playground dust or thudding on asphalt. But the words. . . .

> *Outsider inside*
> *One and two*
> *Run to me*
> *Out of the blue.*
> *Outsider inside*
> *Run some more*
> *Wait for the grunter*
> *Three and four.*
> *Outsider jump*
> *On a pig—quick sticks!*

> *Outsider inside*
> *Five and six.*
> *Outsider inside*
> *Don't be late*
> *Hold on very tightly*
> *Seven and eight.*
> *Outsider outside*
> *Home again*
> *Home on a pig's back*
> *Nine and ten!*

Outsider inside! Rachel began to tremble. She was an Outsider inside. Inside this world, trying to get out again! She remembered her own thought on the drive here—a lot of old sayings and rhymes are about true things, but people get used to them and say them without thinking what they mean.

Wait for the grunter the verse said. The grunter—and a Force 10 grunter was rising outside right now! *Outsider jump*

On a pig—quick sticks . . . it was the way home—in an old children's chant. *Home on a pig's back—* on a pig's back. . . .

Rachel wrenched open the truck door, clutching the book. She ran stumbling across the grass in front of the house. But it was too late. The sky was already crowded. The pigs were up. All the pigs were up! The last grunter of the season, Bert had said, and she'd missed her chance.

"No!" cried Rachel, and she could hardly hear her own voice, so loud was the grunting and squealing, like thunder in the air, so wild was the wind that had sprung up, buffeting the pigs, whipping her hair.

She looked around desperately, straining her eyes against the sun and the wind.

And then she saw it—one big pig—an enormous pig, its ears fluttering like sails, standing

proudly alone on the hillside. The grandfather of all pigs, waiting his turn to fly.

Rachel tripped on her slippers and nearly fell. She kicked them off and shoved the precious book underneath them. That would have to be her message to Bert and Enid. They'd see them, and surely they'd know. . . .

She began to run up the grassy slope, half climbing, stumbling in the tufty grass. A tingling feeling began to run all over her body, and at the same moment the great pig lifted its nose in the air and snorted, and all the other pigs began to squeal and grunt and roll, rising higher and higher. UEF 10! She could feel it. It was all around her—in the air, in the grass, in her hair, on her skin.

"Wait!" screamed Rachel against the wind. And the pig turned its great head to look as its body shuddered and it began, slowly, to drift.

"Wait! Please wait! Oh!" With a cry Rachel stumbled and fell, sprawling on the prickly tussocks. She buried her face in the grass. She'd never make it now. A wave of misery swept up and covered her.

Her hands groped in front of her and closed on something hard. It was her drink bottle from home. She'd found her yellow drink bottle, still lying in the grass where it had fallen during that terrifying unicorn gallop the day before. Its white cap lay beside it.

Rachel scrambled up, clutching the bottle, clipping the cap on tightly, ignoring her scraped hands, her aching chest. She *would* get home. She *would*.

And Rachel ran, as she'd never run before. She ran gasping and calling, and the great pig called back. She could see its little wise eyes now, and the fringes of hair on its ears. She saw its feet clear the grass tips.

Then, she was beside it, arms stretched high, desperately trying to get a grip. The pig grunted. It was now or never.

She jumped, slipping on the animal's silky hair. She jumped again, with all her strength, and this time her hands found a grip on the huge neck. She clambered up on the pig's back and held on. No time to be frightened or wonder what was going to happen next, to think about Enid, or Bert, or even home. The UEF had them. And with a low rumble of happiness, Rachel's pig soared upward, released at last into the dazzling sky.

The world spun beneath them, and all around

was blue. They climbed higher and higher, and the wind whistled around their ears, pulling at Rachel's aching arms, whipping her hair.

She could hardly see through her streaming eyes.

"Hold on!" she begged herself. "Hold on!"

But even as she whispered the words, there was a blast of rushing warm air and the great pig was swept up in a dizzying spiral. Rachel felt her stinging eyes closing, her hands loosening their grip, her legs sliding over the silky hair. A ringing began in her ears. The pig snorted, tossed, somersaulted—and Rachel was falling. . . .

Pigs Might Fly!

Rachel opened her eyes and, for a moment, hardly dared to believe it. She lay flat on the bed, her heart beating wildly, her arms and legs aching. She shook her head. The ringing in her ears was still there. But this was her room. Her bed. She was home. Somewhere up there in the blue air she'd broken through. She was back Outside. Home.

She heard her mother's footsteps in the hall downstairs. Of course—that was the doorbell she could hear.

"Mum! Dad!" She tried to yell, but her throat was sore, and she found the shout turned into a croak. She wanted to see them, tell them she was back, be hugged and kissed and fussed over. Then she'd know it was really true—that it was all over, and she really was safe at home again. She lay still, listening, and for the first time noticed that it was still raining.

"Hold on!" called Alice, as if this was just an ordinary day, and opened the front door.

Rachel listened carefully.

"Sandy—back again! What's up? . . . What? Of course she's all right. . . . Of course you can, but, Sandy, it's only a little cold. . . . Okay, I'll see you later. I'll just finish . . ."

Footsteps pounded on the stairs. Sandy was coming up two at a time. Rachel lay quietly, waiting.

The steps slowed, began to tiptoe. Sandy appeared at the door. His coat was wet, his face pale and anxious. He peeped in as though he was scared of what he might find. Then he saw her, and with a bound he was across the room, grinning, all trace of strain gone.

"Oh, Rachel! Boy—I was so . . ." he began, and then made a visible effort to calm himself down. "Oh," he said, in a casual-sounding voice. "I just thought I'd pop in and—and—see you again, on my way home. When I visited earlier I . . ."

"Earlier? Oh—thanks," said Rachel, confused. So—so somehow her time Inside hadn't counted here. She hadn't lost any time at all.

"And—ah—while I'm here," gabbled Sandy, "I may as well just take away this rubbishy little sketch I did this morning—um . . ." He reached over and almost snatched the little picture from its place on the bedside table. He crushed it into his pocket. "Ah—I've got a funnier idea for a picture for you—you'll like it a lot better." He wiped his forehead. His hands were trembling a little.

Suddenly everything clicked into place for Rachel.

"You're puffed!" she said, watching him intently.

"Yes, I . . . I decided to jog home. For exercise."

"It wouldn't have been because of the picture, would it?" Rachel teased.

"Because? . . ."

"Because of the picture you drew and left for me to look at? I mean, it wasn't because you suddenly thought it might be—um—sort of—dangerous?"

Sandy stared at her openmouthed.

Chris appeared at the door.

"Daddy!" Rachel held out her arms and he came over to her. She felt his strong arms around her and put her head on his chest, gratefully rubbing her cheek against the roughness of his old sweater.

"You're a cuddlepot this morning," he said, and patted her back. "Do you feel sick?"

"No. No. I'm so happy!"

"Funny old thing you are," he said, smiling at her. Then he wrinkled his nose. "Funny smell in here, isn't there? Sort of barnyardy. Maybe you need a bath, darling."

"Dad!"

"Well, just a thought." He gave her a final pat and stood up. "See you downstairs, Sandy."

"Right, mate. Five minutes," said Sandy, smiling weakly, one eye on Rachel.

"Dad, did you know that Sandy's short for Alexander?" said Rachel sweetly.

Chris looked at her in surprise. "Er—yes—I know that, darling. Why?"

"Oh—I only just found out. Do you know what Sandy used to do, before he was a sign writer?"

"Ah—an accountant, wasn't it, mate?"

"A bank teller, actually," said Sandy, and began

to smile. "I decided I liked fiddling around with paints better."

"Yeah, that's right. Are you two having a careers discussion or something?"

"More or less," said Sandy, stroking his beard.

"Well, I'll see you down there. Okay?"

"Okay."

Chris grinned at them and left the room.

There was silence as he clattered down the stairs.

Sandy sat down abruptly on the end of the bed.

"I'm speechless!" he said. "Rachel . . ."

Rachel laughed. "I was there," she whispered. "I met Mr. Murray, the bank manager, and Cathy Titterton, and lots of other people. They remembered you. And then I found the book. Your book, with . . ."

"With the kids' rhymes in it? It took me six months. How did? . . ."

"Miss Coolie helped me."

"Connie Coolie—oh—oh, my fur and feathers, what a stroke of luck!"

"I followed the rhyme, and I got back."

Sandy was pale. "Oh, Rachel, I don't know what to say. If I'd known. . . . That picture . . . I'd never have . . . I mean, what if you hadn't found the book?"

"I don't know," said Rachel seriously. "I don't suppose time stands still here forever. If I hadn't worked it out . . ."

They stared at one another.

"Still," said Rachel, flinging out her hands. "I *did* work it out and I *did* get home. I was so scared—but it was so exciting, too."

Sandy nodded. "I know what you mean," he said. "I still can't . . ."

"And now," said Rachel mischievously, "I understand why such interesting things happen to you all the time. I'd always wondered. Miss Coolie told me how you stole her thermos!"

"I didn't steal it!" protested Sandy. "I left money for it. I needed it to . . ." He paused.

"To collect your own supply of UEF and bring it home!"

Sandy cast his hands helplessly into the air.

"Sprung!" he grinned. "You're right. I just let a bit out, now and then, when life's dull, just to make it a bit more . . ."

"Unlikely?" giggled Rachel.

"Yeah." Sandy smiled at her. "I'd always planned to do that—take some with me—and Connie's thermos was the only container I could lay my hands on. I had to leave so quickly. Pigs up all over the place, and I wasn't going to miss my chance."

He leaned forward. "Mind you," he said, "I'm not the only Outsider to have brought some back, I'm sure of that. I mean, according to what I read Inside, there've been Outsiders visiting there for centuries. Most of them seem to have got back Outside somehow or other. And I'm positive that I'm not the first to think of the advantages of a little store of UEF back home. I mean, history's full of people who seem to have had a stronger than normal belief in the Unlikely Event."

"Yes . . ." said Rachel. "You know that man who's just flown around the world in a helicopter? I was wondering . . ."

"A very possible candidate!" exclaimed Sandy.

"UEF Force 10," said Rachel dreamily. "Pure Force 10."

"Yeah," grinned Sandy, "it's powerful stuff. I've had mine ten years, and it still hasn't run out."

"Great!" Rachel leaned back on her pillows. She put her hand under the bedclothes and drew out a yellow plastic bottle.

Sandy leaped to his feet, eyes wide.

"Don't tell me!" he yelled.

Rachel nodded. "I didn't mean to take it—it just happened. It was lying open on the grass, and I put the cap on without thinking and brought it with me."

"Is it? . . ."

Rachel nodded again.

"UEF Force 10. Pure Force 10," she said.

Sandy clapped his hand over his mouth. "Two lots of UEF in one street!" he said. "We'll have to be careful." He thought a moment, and then he began to grin.